092181

Kaminsky, Stuart M.

Tomorrow is another
day.

$18.95

DATE			

TOMORROW·IS ANOTHER·DAY

TOMORROW·IS ANOTHER·DAY

STUART M. KAMINSKY

THE MYSTERIOUS PRESS

Published by Warner Books

A Time Warner Company

Mysterious Press books are published by Warner Books, Inc.,
1271 Avenue of the Americas, New York, NY 10020.

A Time Warner Company

The Mysterious Press name and logo are registered trademarks of Warner Books, Inc.

Printed in the United States of America

First Printing: February 1995

10 9 8 7 6 5 4 3 2 1

Library of Congress Cataloging-in-Publication Data

Kaminsky, Stuart M.
    Tomorrow is another day / Stuart M. Kaminsky.
       p.   cm.
    ISBN 0-89296-527-4 :
    1. Peters, Toby (Fictitious character)—Fiction. 2. Motion
picture actors and actresses—California—Los Angeles—Fiction.
3. Private investigators—California—Los Angeles—Fiction.
4. Hollywood (Los Angeles, Calif.)—Fiction. 5. Gable, Clark,
1901-1960—Fiction. [1. Gone with the wind (Motion picture)-
-Fiction.] I. Title.
PS3561. A43T66   1995
813' .54—dc20   94-18987
                                                          CIP

*To Hawley Rogers, the faculty
and the students of Oldfields School*

Prologue

Atlanta was burning on the back lot of Selznick International.

Cameras were grinding while walls and fake storefronts of old sets from *King of Kings, King Kong, Garden of Allah,* which had been doctored to look like Atlanta, at least from a distance, went up in crackling fire.

"Looks like what Hitler's doing in Czechoslovakia," Wally Hospodar, second-in-command, Selznick International security, said to me.

I shrugged and watched the darkness beyond the half acre of burning set.

Wally had hired a dozen backup private detectives, and security guards with studio experience like me had been hired for one night of work and the promise of more on *Gone With the Wind*.

Atlanta was burning with seven technicolor cameras grinding all over the place till they got it right. The studio had its own fire department, but more than two hundred studio employees had been given a crash fire-fighting course and were standing by while the Culver City fire chief, Ernest Grey, tried to control them and all of his own men and trucks.

It was a security nightmare. A stray fan in a U.S.C. sweater, a guy with a grudge against Selznick or old man Mayer, could get in the middle of the shot and force Selznick to rebuild Atlanta and burn it all over again. As it was, the fire had been started seven times and stopped seven times and started again where the second-unit director, Bill Menzies, wanted some extra coverage.

The air was hot, sticky, and smelled of smoke. Reporters who had heard, from carefully planted phone calls from Selznick's press people, particularly Russell Birdwell, that the back lot in Culver City was on fire were trying to talk their way past a detail of security guards. A mile away on Washington Street, Louis B. Mayer and his office staff were probably watching the smoking skies and worrying about the investment they had made in what Selznick had promised would be the biggest movie ever made.

Time and money were on the line, not to mention the embarrassment if the long-delayed Movie of the Century had to close down at the start of shooting.

"Wall back there," Wally said, nodding to the right. "That's the one on Skull Island, kept Kong out. I hear that's Hitler's favorite movie."

I grunted, the heat warming my face. Wally was a good guy, ready for retirement, fond of the bottle, full of information about the movies, and obsessed with the daily movements of Adolph Hitler who, Wally insisted, his sagging jowly face nodding, would soon attack all of Europe and pull us into a war.

We were about a dozen yards behind David O. Selznick, who was wearing a helmet and had already gone hoarse from shouting directions through a megaphone from a spindly tower that had been built so he could see every camera and actor, and most of the forty acres of lot stretching into the early-morning darkness. Behind us, George Cukor, director of the movie, was sitting on a chair, whispering to a thin young guy I didn't recognize. Cukor was staying out of the way while the burning of Atlanta was directed by William Cameron Menzies. It was an action shoot, a second-unit job made harder by Selznick's taking over.

"The wagon," Selznick shouted, pacing and smoking a cigarette at the foot of his tower. "Where's the wagon?"

The wagon was off to the right, in darkness. Wally and I had been there when Dorothy Fargo and Yakima Canutt, dressed like Scarlett O'Hara and Rhett Butler, had gone over the action with Menzies and his assistant. Yak had been around forever, a lean, board-hard man with a dark Indian face, as much the king of stunt men as Clark Gable was king of Hollywood.

"Mame Stoltz in publicity, you know Mame?" Wally asked, while I tried to do my job. "Mame says Paulette Goddard's out as Scarlett. Too Jewish, something. Who knows? Start a picture you don't have a star. Bad luck. Not that I'm fool enough to tell anybody that. Been here since Ince owned the studio, made it through Goldwyn, Pathé, and R.K.O. And I'm hanging on with Selznick. You know why I'm hanging on?"

"You're not fool enough to give advice," I said.

"Precisely," said Wally, pulling out a pouch of Dill's Best and filling his pipe. "Exactly, precisely."

I grunted in understanding. Wally had gotten me on this job and assigned me to work with him on the detail guarding Selznick and the crew. Easy work. And I needed the money. I also wanted to meet Clark Gable. I'd only seen him once before from a distance when I tried to keep fans from Mickey Rooney at an M-G-M premiere at Grauman's Chinese.

I've been around Hollywood for all of my almost fifty years. Stars didn't impress me, except for Jimmy Stewart, Buck Jones, and Gable. I'd heard a lot about Gable, some good, some bad, and I wanted to know how much of it was true. But more important, I was getting paid.

The flames and smoke of the burning set were climbing high into the sky over Los Angeles, and Selznick was in near panic. He took off his helmet, brushed back his gray tight curls, and looked at Menzies.

"Bill," he pleaded.

"Action," Menzies said softly to his assistant, who relayed the order on his phone.

A guy in uniform, Confederate gray, wearing a beard and covered with make-believe dust moved next to us. The lot was full of these war-weary extras. Around like popcorn for when the assistant director needed a soldier or eighty soldiers with three minutes' notice from Selznick or one of the directors.

"Hell of a night," the man said.

I didn't look at him. I was watching Yak and Dotty Fargo race onto the burning set on their bucking cart.

"Next few days," the man at my side said, "I lie out there and pretend I'm dying. Doesn't look like I'll even get a line, but who knows. You need pull, clout, a break, and who do I know, I ask you?"

"That's the way of it," said Wally.

"Should have been me," the man next to me said. "You know I tested for Rhett Butler? I've got the look, the accent, but not the credits. I heard them talking. Gable backs out and they maybe go with me. Why not? Big publicity push. Star is born. Character actor Lionel Varney gets the break he deserves."

"Don't miss any of this, any of this," Selznick was saying more to himself than to Menzies or to Ray Rennahan, who was coordinating the cameras.

The cart with Yak and Dotty was almost across the set now. No turning back. No reshooting.

"No problems. No problems," Selznick muttered.

"It can break a man's heart, his spirit. You know?" Varney said at my side.

"Tough business," I said.

"Wasn't for Gable I'd be trying on white hats with big brims, smoking thin cigars, paying my bills with cash, kissing Paulette Goddard in front of the cameras," said Varney. "I'm a better actor."

"I heard Goddard's out," I said, wondering if the gaffer off camera far to the left was moving forward onto the set. I nudged Wally, who looked where I was pointing.

"I know him," said Wally. "No problem there."

"Gable's fault," Varney said. "He doesn't need this movie. He's the king. I need it. And instead of wearing fancy clothes, I'll be dying in dirty gray down there tomorrow. Is that fair or is that fair?"

It was typical Hollywood feel-sorry-for-myself, I'm-a-better-actor-than-Paul-Muni banter, but Varney was spilling it to a stranger, a stranger who had been hired to keep people with grudges and a passion for publicity from damaging the biggest movie ever made.

The cart cleared the set and rumbled into the darkness.

"It's fine," called Menzies, and the word was relayed. "Keep rolling till we have no more flames."

People cheered and Selznick turned, his face red from the heat of the still-burning set.

I turned to look at Varney but he was a few dozen yards away now, his back to me, walking away with sagging shoulders. I took a step toward him. A man and woman brushed past Varney, almost bumping into him. The man and woman were headed straight for Selznick. I nudged Wally, who turned.

"Selznick's brother, Myron, the agent," he said. "Looks like he's had a few under his belt tonight."

"He supposed to be on the set?" I asked.

"You wanna tell him to go away? Step in and make a mistake and you'll be looking for short-order work in Topeka," Wally said.

I moved closer to Selznick just in case. Varney had now disappeared.

David O. Selznick didn't see his brother and the girl for an instant. He had turned back to light a cigarette and watch the flames consume what was left of the Atlanta set.

"David," Myron said.

"Went without a hitch, Myron. Without a hitch," Selznick said with a sigh, turning to face his brother. "Did you see?"

"David," Myron said, looking in the flickering light like a Freddy March about to turn into Mr. Hyde. "I'd like you to meet Scarlett O'Hara."

Selznick turned now and looked down at the young woman. He took her hand and grinned at his brother, probably more happy with having the scene successfully in the can than with the prospect of Myron having discovered a last-minute Scarlett after two years of searching and screen tests of every actress in Hollywood, with the possible exception of Mae West.

"Vivien Leigh," said Myron, and Vivien Leigh, her small, pale hand in David Selznick's large one, smiled.

"Hear that?" Wally said at my side.

There was noise all around. Fire trucks. Cranes, trucks, the voices of people congratulating each other.

"What?" I asked.

"Come on," he said, touching my shoulder.

I followed Wally away from the meeting between the Selznicks and Leigh. He ran down a gully on his spindly legs and hurried into a stand of bushes. I went after him into the darkness. Now I could hear something ahead of us.

Wally plowed ahead until we cleared the trees, went up a little hill, and found ourselves panting and looking at a group of Confederate soldiers who were about thirty yards ahead of us around an open fire.

"He's dead," one of the soldiers shouted. "I've seen dead. He's dead."

Wally pushed ahead and we made our way through the group that included the guy named Varney who had talked to us a few minutes earlier.

When we broke through we saw the dead man, in a gray uniform. He was lying at the bottom of what looked like a drainage ditch. A sword was plunged into his stomach. The sword swayed as if someone had set it in motion.

"Anybody see what happened?" Wally said.

"Just fell on it, I guess," an extra in a gray private's uniform said.

"I saw him fall on it," said Varney, as Wally and I scurried down the side of the ditch toward the dead man.

Wally got down first and kneeled next to the corpse, careful not to touch anything.

"Dead for sure," he said. "First, probably not the last, on a picture this big."

I stood next to him, my trouser cuffs getting wet with mud. I'd see them dead before. Wally got up.

"Picture like this," he went on, reaching for his pipe and tobacco, "no surprise. Bound to be some accidents. Think we had four or five killed on *Ben-Hur* back in the old days. My guess is they'll want to keep this quiet a while. Low key."

I'd seen cover-ups at Warners when I worked security there, had even helped with one or two that would have been the end of rising and falling stars, writers, and directors.

Wally and I looked up to the top of the ditch. The Confederate extras had scurried into the night and the smell of burning sets, but someone was standing in the shadows at the top of the hill. Our eyes met for a second and then Clark Gable, or a hell of a ringer, turned and walked away.

Wally spent the next few hours writing the report and talking to the Culver City Police. The dead man hadn't been carrying identification. His wallet and things were probably in his car, parked in the lot with hundreds of others. The police would find it, check it out, and mark it down as a freak accident. Case closed. Atlanta burned. On to Tara, being built about half a mile away.

I was called early the next afternoon. I was half asleep.

"Toby," said Wally. "Going to have to let you go. I'll see to it you get paid for the week."

"The dead soldier?" I guessed.

"You got it. Powers that be think it best if you and the extras who were around that fire not be here where you might make mention of the incident to a reporter or some gaffer with a big mouth."

"I wouldn't do that, Wally," I said.

"I know you wouldn't, but this way, I don't have to put myself on the line and say so. What do we gain? Nothing. What can I lose? My job. Let's keep it this way. Simple. I'll be looking for more work for you down the line."

"Did you talk to Gable?" I asked.

"Gable?"

"He was there," I said. "Top of the hill when we found the body."

"Not a chance, Toby," he said. "Gable didn't have a call last night and he's not the kind that stands around watching people make movies when he doesn't have to."

"My mistake," I said.

"I'll call you as soon as I've got something for you."

It would be five years before I talked to Wally again.

Chapter 1

Aside from the fact that a giant Samoan named Andy was not standing on the chest of a little man named Charles Westfarland, and the tables and chairs weren't torn and shattered in front of the bandstand, the Mozambique Lounge in Glendale looked pretty much the way it had when I had last been in it almost ten years earlier.

It was early in the evening, Sunday, February 28, 1943, and I had come to see a client who had asked me to meet him at the Mozambique. I said I could, and he had started to give me directions; I cut him off and told him I knew the place, knew it well.

The Mozambique was dark and heavy with the same smell of alcohol and tired lust it had a decade ago. Two couples sat at one of the white-and-red-checkered tables in front of the bandstand, where a bored-looking old guy who looked like Clifton Webb was playing a pretty damned good boogie-woogie version of "There's a Breeze on Lake Louise." At the table next to the two couples, who were laughing like phony extras, a trio of uniformed sailors sat nursing Gobel beers and wondering whether they should pay attention to Clifton Webb or swap prewar stories. Two of the sailors were about ten years old and probably didn't have any stories but the *Three Billy*

Goats Gruff. The third sailor was a lot older. In fact, if he could act, he probably had a good shot at playing Sheridan Whiteside in a road-company production of *The Man Who Came to Dinner*. Seaman Whiteside was doing the talking.

The red-leatherette booths along the wall to my right were empty except for a guy in the far corner, hidden in the shadows and smoking. The bar was long, dark wood shined like a mirror from hell, the pride of Lester Gannett, who owned the place and poured the drinks. I was sure that when I last saw him four years earlier Gannett had been leaning on the bar the way he was now. But back then he hadn't been pouring something amber from a bottle into the tumbler of a little girl made up like someone's bad idea of a lady of the evening. The kid in the army air-corps uniform next to her smiled and looked at Lester in the hope of getting some acknowledgment of his good luck at landing this infant version of Lana Turner.

"Wow," said Sidney, perched just about where he had been a year before the war started. Sidney ruffled his white feathers and closed his beak, looking at me as to one more rich in hope. Sidney was an old cockatoo. The Mozambique was perfect. It even smelled like the jungle.

Lester noticed me. His round head cocked to one side like the old bird next to me, as he tried to place my dark eyes and busted nose.

I walked forward and sat on a stool five down from the painted passion flower playing hooky from eighth grade. Lester slid along behind the bar, bottle in hand, whimsical smile on his face. He looked a little like the moon with pockmarks.

"Officer . . . don't tell me. Let me remember."

"Peters," I said, adjusting my tie in the bar mirror and surveying the room.

"Peters? No, that's not it," said Gannett.

"Pevsner," I said. "I changed it to Peters."

"Right," said Gannett. "Pevsner. I got a memory or what?"

"I get a prize for remembering my own name?"

"Sure thing," said Gannett with a grin. "Name it."

"Beer," I said.

"Suit yourself," he said with a shrug, letting me know that money was no object when it came to someone as important as an ex-cop who could remember his own name. "Been a while."

"About ten years," I said. "I'm not a cop anymore."

Gannett, reaching over to hit the tap handle and fill a mug with beer, kept grinning and pouring.

"That a fact?" he said.

"A fact," I said, watching the foam spill over the side of the mug he placed in front of me on a cardboard coaster. "Want to take the beer back?"

"To your good health," he said with a shrug.

"And yours," I agreed, toasting him and taking a drink.

"So, what you been up to?" he said, figuring maybe that I hadn't just dropped into the Mozambique for old time's sake.

"Worked security at Warner Brothers. Been doing private investigations for a while," I said, downing more beer.

"Tagged you for the army," Gannett said, leaning over and cleaning up the beer spill on his slick bar.

Gannett hadn't tagged me for anything, hadn't even thought about me since Babe Ruth retired from the Boston Braves.

"I'm pushing fifty, Lester," I said.

"No shit," he said, shaking his head. "I'd have said you were thirty-five tops. I'm fifty-two and look it, but you . . ."

I looked at myself in the mirror behind the bar. The face belonged to a middleweight who had gone too many losing rounds at least two decades earlier.

"I'll bet you tell that to all the customers," I said, downing the rest of the beer and eyeing the empty mug.

"Most," Gannett agreed. "Most. Want another?"

This time I shrugged.

"It's on you, Peters," he said. "Old times is old times, but . . ."

I fished out a quarter and plucked it on the bar.

The piano guy who looked like Clifton Webb finished his song and two people applauded politely, the kid with the infant hooker and the old sailor. The piano player nodded and launched into "Moonlight and Roses."

One night back when I was a Glendale cop, my partner Matt and I took a call about a fight in the Mozambique. Matt was a wheezer thinking about retiring to a small orange grove near Lompoc. I was a guy with a wife and gun.

The fight was over when we got there. A guy as big as a red Los Angeles trolley with an unsmiling flat face was standing on the stomach of a decidedly smaller guy who wasn't moving and may not have been breathing. They were right in front of the bandstand. Tables and chairs were overturned and any customers who might have been around five minutes earlier were all on their way home to listen to Stoopnagle and Bud.

"He's a Samoan," Lester Gannett had whispered to us from behind the bar.

"The big guy or the one on the floor?" I asked.

"Big guy," he said. "Other one's Charlie Westfarland or something like that. Welsh, Irish. Something. Who knows?"

"Helpful information," I said, while my partner tipped his blue cap back and sat at the bar, facing the path of destruction to the bandstand.

"Little guy, Charlie, thought Andy was a Jap," Lester explained. "Said something. You know. Harmless. And Andy goes stark nuts."

"Big guy?" I asked.

"Big guy," Gannett confirmed. "Been coming in for a week. On a construction job, something over near the cemetery. Who knows? Will you just get him the hell out of here?

Night crowd'll be coming soon and I got a singer. It's Friday, you know. I got a singer, Fridays."

"Give you seven to four the Samoan falls off the other guy inside a minute," said my partner.

I looked at the two men among the mess of broken chairs and scattered tables. The big Samoan, a dreamy look in his eyes, was riding the unconscious guy as if he were a log.

"Matt," I said. "Little guy might be dead."

Matt touched his chin, thought for a beat, and said, "Even money. Take dead or alive. Your pick."

I'd left him sitting there trying to make the same bet with Gannett, who seemed to be considering it seriously.

"Andy," I had said, my hands folded in front of me as I approached the Samoan, my best Officer Gently smile on my face. "What've we got here?"

Andy returned from Oz and looked at me with no expression. He just kept rocking on little Charlie's bigoted chest.

"Well," I said. "I'd say we've got a situation."

Andy reached up and scratched his thick neck.

"I'd say you'd better step off the very quiet gentleman so I can see if he's alive."

Andy stopped scratching and continued to eye me, as if I were about to do something that might interest him. I looked back at the bar. Matt had laid some bills on it. Gannett was matching them as he watched us.

"They're betting on whether I'm going to have to shoot you," I said.

Andy turned his head away as if I were boring him, and I lost eye contact. A very bad sign.

"I've never shot anybody, Andy," I said softly. "Don't want to. Look, I don't know you. You don't know me. Fella you're standing on is probably a son of a bitch who deserves a good beating. He's got that. You wind up on trial for murder and you both get more than you deserve."

Andy was either listening or tiring. He stopped rocking on the fallen guy's stomach and almost fell. Someone behind me, probably Gannett, gasped, his bet in jeopardy.

"Aw, the hell with this," said Matt, who'd come up behind me. He pushed past, kicking the remains of a chair out of the way. Matt stepped up to Andy, who with the added ten inches of the fallen guy's body was about twenty feet tall. Matt hit the big guy full and hard in the face with his night stick.

The bonk of oak against bone echoed through the painted jungle of the Mozambique and Andy toppled backward onto the stage, his nose split. Sidney the cockatoo screamed "Wow."

"Bet's off," shouted Gannett. "You knocked him off."

Matt stepped over the little guy on the floor and onto the bandstand, where he gave the motionless Andy a second bonk on the head. I kneeled over the little guy and put my ear to his chest. Something was rattling in there besides broken ribs.

"Resisting arrest," Matt had wheezed, trying to turn Andy over. "Give me a hand turning this fat Jap over so I can cuff him."

"He's Samoan," I said, and turned to Gannett to shout, "Call an ambulance."

"Wow," Sidney screamed again.

"It's no fun anymore, Tobias," Matt said as we turned Andy over on his stomach.

"I know what you mean," I'd said.

Six months later I had traded my Glendale blues for Warner Brothers greens. Now I was back in Glendale, back at the Mozambique, and looking for my client.

I was fresh off a job with a few dollars left. I'd cleared enough to pay Mrs. Plaut a month's rent, get my clothes repaired and buy a new Windbreaker at Hy's for Him, and have No-Neck Arnie bring my Crosley back to life, including a new door and a patchwork transmission. I'd also cleared enough to take Carmen, the ample cashier at Levy's on Spring Street, to two dinners, a Jimmy Wakely triple-feature, and an all-night Wrestle-Rama at the Garden. In gratitude for this lavishness I had received two generous wet kisses, a momentary left hand between my legs while I was driving her home, and an invitation to a taco dinner at the apartment she shared with her eleven-year-old son who in his kinder moments called me Wolfman.

I needed work and a fresh start.

I needed the new client in the shadows of the red-leatherette booth, who had told me to meet him at the Mozambique.

"Guy in the booth," I said to Gannett without turning my head from my drink. "How long's he been here?"

"Ten, fifteen minutes maybe," Gannett answered. "He's four ahead of you. He your old partner?"

"Why?" I asked.

"Looks familiar," said Gannett. "And looks like he's spoiling for something. So if you boys are bringing trouble, I'll ask you to find another bar. No skin off my ass either way. Know what I mean?"

"Seems clear enough to me," I said, getting off the stool.

"That's my motto," Gannett said, moving down to the army air-corps kid who was buying Herbert Tarryton's and paying for cheap bourbon for himself and the painted girl. She was holding up a hell of a lot better than he was.

"Can you move it, pops?" the tipsy air-corps kid said, waving a five-dollar bill toward Gannett. "Lady's thirsty."

"She can hold her liquor," I said.

"Seems that way," Gannett said, meeting my eyes.

"I'd say she was maybe fifteen, sixteen tops," I whispered.

"Just turned sixteen," Gannett whispered back.

"Pops," the young man rasped and then seemed to forget what he was going to say.

"She's cute," I said to Gannett behind the bar.

"Me and her mom think so," said Gannett.

I nodded. "Your kid?"

"Family business," he said. "Lillian, that's the wife, is too old for it. Bad legs, those veins you know. Varicose. Hard for her to stand and, let's face it, the looks go."

"Family business," I echoed.

"Jeannie's drinkin' tea from a bourbon bottle," he whispered, nodding at his daughter and ignoring the boy in the air-corps uniform. "She only works two, three nights a week. She's a good kid, she is. Good student. Glendale High. Sophomore. Thinking of going to Stanford if the grades hold up."

"You must be proud of her," I said.

"I am," said Gannett, the barkeep smile gone. "If you're really undercover, you've got nothing here."

"No skin off my ass either way," I said.

"Hey, pops," the young airman shouted over the piano, "you gonna wait on us or do we walk?"

"You want another beer on the house?" Gannett said to me as he held up a hand to quiet the kid.

"No, thanks," I said, turning toward the booths along the wall.

"Talent's all gone downtown," Gannett said behind me. "The fleet's always in. The troops are always shipping out. Girls go where the money is. Family man has to make a living."

The piano man was dourly humming "I Want To Be Happy" to the keys of his piano as I inched past the two couples at the table.

One of the men, a guy with short gray hair, said, ". . . and Abie says . . . he says . . ." The guy was choking with tears of laughter as he said in what he thought sounded like the voice of an old Jew, "So vot vould you vant from me, I should pay him cash?"

The other man and the two women at the table broke up. One of them slapped the table.

"Pay him ca . . ." one of the women gasped. "Oh, Frank."

One of the young sailors at the next table had picked up the tail end of the joke. He didn't find it funny. I would have given my old partner seven to four that the young sailor was named something like Bernstein and that he was now waiting for an anti-Semitic punch line. The automatic sensor on the back of my neck was ready to distance me and my potential client from a scene that might make Andy the Samoan's body-rolling act four years ago look like amateur night at St. Anne's Church.

I slid into the dark booth across from the man, who took a drag on his cigarette. The glow showed a familiar but slightly heavier and much more serious face than the one I had expected.

"Peters?" he said.

"Peters," I confirmed, holding out my hand. He took it.

Clark Gable was dressed in a long-sleeved black pullover shirt. His hair, graying at more than the temples, was cut military short.

"Where've we met before?" he asked in a manner that could only be viewed as hostile.

"Four years ago. Hearst Castle. I interviewed you about a case I was working."

"Yes, I remember now."

"And before that," I said. "First day of shooting on *Gone With the Wind*. I was working security. An extra got killed, fell on his sword. You were there."

"Yeah," said Gable. "I remember that night. I stayed out of the way, talked to a few people on the crew, some extras. Then that guy got killed. Don't remember you, though."

"I've got one of those faces."

"Okay, enough small talk. What are you pulling here?" Gable asked as I settled back in the booth.

"Pulling?"

"I don't respond to blackmail or threats," Gable said, trying to control himself. "And I don't have much left in the way of patience or understanding."

"I'm missing something here," I said.

The piano player rolled "Anything Goes" to a gentle flourish and applause from Lester's daughter.

"Wow," Sidney cried from the bar.

"Thank you, lady and bird," the piano player said wearily as Gable handed me a folded piece of paper. I spread it and read the typed poem:

> They die until you understand,
> They die by weapons in my hand.
> My father wept to be so cut
> From fortune, fame deservéd, but
> I'll avenge the wrongs and slight
> To be there e'er the Ides and right
> Those wrongs and claim his prize
> And give to you a great surprise.
> First there was Charles Larkin
> And next Al Ramone. Do harken
> For on it goes and blood be thine
> Unless you learn to read my s.i.g.n.

When I'd finished, I looked up at Gable, whose hands were folded on the table in front of him.

"Turn it over," he said.

I turned it over. My name and address were printed in the same ink and same handwriting as the poem. I looked up at Gable, as the piano player said without enthusiasm: "And now, direct from appearances on the 'Voice of Firestone' and

major roles in such movies as *They Got Me Covered* and *Gone
With the Wind* . . ."

"You don't get it, do you?" Gable said, his eyes narrow, unblinking.

I started to speak but Gable nodded toward the bandstand.
I looked toward the piano player, who was saying, ". . . San
Fernando Valley's answer to Bing Crosby, Nelson Eddy, and
Russ Columbo all rolled into baritone—Alan Ramone."

More applause from Lester's kid, Jeanne. Frank at the next
table, who had just launched into another Jewish joke, low-
ered his voice.

Alan Ramone, wrinkled suit, carrying about thirty pounds
more than his fighting weight, wearing one of the worst hair-
pieces outside of Hollywood, walked onto the stage. His face
was powdered. His teeth were even and false. He nodded in
appreciation of his fabulous introduction and the nonexistent
applause.

As the singer moved to the unnecessary microphone at the
edge of the bandstand, Gable produced a newspaper clipping
and slid it toward me. I laid it on top of the poem. It was
from the *Los Angeles Times*, dated February 21, a week ago. The
piano player ruffled the keys and Alan Ramone's less than
solid flesh and more-than-faltering voice launched into a medley of tunes from *Show Boat*.

The article was simple, an announcement of the death of
one Charles Larkin in a freak accident, a fall in his Culver City
apartment. There were no details. Larkin was forty-three. He
was an actor and May Company salesman who had been seen
in such films as *Bittersweet*, *Dames*, and *Gone With the Wind*.

"I'm in the States for a week," said Gable evenly, as Alan
Ramone forgot the words to "Old Man River" and hummed
through till he came to a place he vaguely remembered.

"Consulting with some people in town on the recruiting

film I'm working on," Gable went on. Ramone raised his volume to gravel out, "He just keeps rolling along."

Since Lester's kid was deep in animated conversation with the soldier, and Sidney was deep into his birdseed, the sailors felt it their patriotic duty to applaud and keep up the morale of a guy who was doing his best to entertain the troops.

"Only a few people I trust knew I was coming back to the States for a few days, but when I get home, this is waiting for me."

"I don't get it," I said.

"I was hoping you did," Gable answered.

Frank's voice rose at the next table. As the applause and Alan Ramone's bow ended, he finished his joke: "Who said kike? I said Spike."

One of the women and the other man at the table laughed. The remaining woman giggled and said, "Oh, Frank," to show how naughty he was being.

"How about shutting up?" the young sailor at the next table said.

Gable shook his head and unfolded his hands.

"Yeah," said Frank, looking up at Alan Ramone with more than a touch of eighty proof in his voice. "You should shut up. You're singin' so loud my friends can't hear each other."

Fresh whoops of laughter.

Alan Ramone did his best to ignore the show below him and nodded at the piano player, who gave him an intro to "Tea for Two."

"I used to think jokes like that were funny," Gable said.

Frank was glancing around to see if anyone besides his pals appreciated his humor.

"What do you make of this?" I said, tapping the clipping and the poem.

"I don't know," said Gable, reaching for his nearly finished drink. "I told you. I was hoping you did. I do know that poor excuse for a baritone we're trying not to listen to may be in danger."

"Why?" I asked.

Gable shook his head as Ramone belted, ". . . to see us or hear us."

"I haven't the slightest idea," said Gable.

"We will raise a family," Ramone rasped.

Gable turned to listen.

"A boy for you. A girl for me."

Gable's eyes were moist.

"Can't you see how happy we will be," Ramone concluded.

I'd done my homework on Gable before this meeting. Yes, I'd met him once before. But that was a different Clark Gable, a smiling, handsome Gable in a bathing suit, with a look of amusement on his face. The Clark Gable across from me—a year after the death of his wife, his mother-in-law, and his best friend in a plane crash in Nevada—was about twenty years older and not amused. Gable and Carole Lombard had been married for a little over two years when she was killed coming back from a trip to the east to sell war bonds. Word had it that Gable had pushed Lombard to go on the war-bond tours, that Lombard was afraid of flying. Word had it that Gable felt more than a little responsible for his wife's death, which maybe explained why Gable had joined the army air corps as a private and had moved up quickly to captain, flying combat missions as a machine gunner and trying to get himself killed. All this was according to a publicity gal named Mame Stoltz, who had been with Selznick and was now at M-G-M.

"Put a candle in your butt and blow it out," Frank shouted drunkenly, failing to come up to his established high level of humor. Nevertheless, his party laughed politely.

The young sailor stood up. His two friends stood up. The old sailor had a wild look in his eye and a smile on his face. Frank and his friend stood up. They were both big.

"You're a detective?"

"Right."

"I've got a job for you. Keep Ramone alive and find out what the hell is going on," Gable said, apparently ignoring the coming Battle of Mozambique. "I don't want to be responsible for any more innocent people dying. You can bill me for your time. This should hold you for a few days."

He slid a white envelope toward me. His name with no address was printed in the upper-left-hand corner. The envelope wasn't sealed. I opened it and found four new fifties. I pushed them back into the envelope and shoved it in my pocket. I would probably have taken the case for nothing but curiosity and to please the sad king across from me. Why was my name on the back of the poem? And what kind of nut sends poems to movie stars he plans to murder?

"I'll take a little break now," Al Ramone said, though he had sung only three songs. "And I'll be back with a medley of your favorite show tunes."

Al was dripping with sweat and fear as he and the piano player retreated stage left.

"Hold it there," called Lester from behind the bar.

Nobody held anything. The sailors took a step toward Frank and his partner. The ladies remained seated and tried not to giggle.

"Why not go to the cops?" I asked Gable.

"If you have to," he said. "If you have to. But only if you have to. It's taken me a year to get lost. A year. I don't want reporters hounding me. I . . . if you have to."

Gable's fingers were playing with what looked like a locket dangling from a chain on his neck. A chair slid backward behind me and I had one of those flashes of having been here before.

"All right. No trouble. There's a cop in here," called Lester, pointing at me.

"I'm a cop too," said Frank, glaring at me. "Who are you?"

"An ex. I'm civilian," I said, holding my hands up.

"Who's your sister?" the other guy with Frank said.

Gable sighed, shook his head, and dug something out of his pocket as he stood up.

"My home phone," he said, handing me a card. "I'll be there."

The sailors had stopped when they heard the word *cop*, and the air-corps kid at the bar had disappeared with Lester's child.

"Son of a bitch," said Frank, looking at Gable as he stepped out of the shadow of the booth. "It's Robert Taylor."

"No," said one of the women. "He's Clark Gable's grandpa."

The other woman laughed.

Gable was almost as big as the two cops and in better shape.

"Call me," said Gable evenly.

"I'll call," I said, pocketing poem, clip, and envelope as Gable turned to the sailors and said, "Gentlemen, I suggest we retire for the evening."

"Gentlemen, I suggest we retire for the evening," Frank mocked drunkenly, stepping in front of Gable, who tried to move past him toward the door.

"That does it," Lester shouted. "That does it. I'm calling the police."

"Wow," screeched Sidney.

Gable and Frank, who was a half-head taller, were face to face.

"Got something else cute to say?" Frank said, winking at the ladies.

"You," said Gable, "are a foul-mouthed sack of horse shit. Now, if you'll step out of my way, I'll leave the trough to you and your friends."

I was halfway across the room now, heading toward the

dark hole to the left of the stage where Al Ramone and the piano player had disappeared. I stopped when I heard Gable and turned to see him rub his nose with his right hand, take a deep breath, and throw a solid right to Frank's stomach, followed by a left to his kidney as the big man spun to his side. One woman gasped. The other screamed. Frank's partner went for Gable but the old sailor was on his back.

I went through the heavy curtain as everyone in the bar—Lester, sailors, women, and cops—screamed and started breaking furniture and each other.

There wasn't much light backstage at the Mozambique, but there wasn't much to see either. A dirty wooden floor. A door with an exit sign over it. Three other unmarked wooden doors and a sputtering light bulb to guide the way.

I went for the first door, opened it, and found myself in a closet set up like a dressing room. Just enough space for a small table and chair and a peeling mirror. Table, chair, and mirror frame had all been painted a sick, thick, and uneven green. The room was empty except for the furniture and a photo tucked into the corner of the mirror. I took a look at the scratched photo. A group of guys in Confederate uniforms were lying on the ground and holding up their hands to Vivien Leigh, begging. One of the guys was circled in ink. He was lying in the dirt, his hands crossed in death. He was skinny and bearded, but Al Ramone's fake teeth gave him away. I looked at the photograph for another few seconds and had the feeling that I had seen this lost patrol before.

A motorcycle cranked up outside. I moved to the open window and pushed the dirty curtain aside in time to see Clark Gable roar into the Glendale night. Behind him and me the battle raged on.

I left the room and tried the next door. It was a closet that smelled of something strong and acrid.

That left one door next to the exit. I pushed through and

found myself facing a sink ringed with brown-yellow stains. The faucet dripped. There were two toilet stalls. One was open and needed flushing. The other was closed.

"Ramone?" I said, looking down at the pair of feet below the closed stall's door. Someone's pants were down, and his pale, hairy ankles were showing.

No answer. The battle continued to rage in the lounge of the Mozambique, but I could barely hear it as I pushed open the stall and found Al Ramone sitting there, his hairpiece in his lap, his teeth pushing forward against his pursed lips, his sagging suit supporting a sagging rod of dark metal that had skewed him to the papered wall. He had looked better as a dead Confederate soldier than as a dead crooner.

I stood over Al Ramone for a few seconds before reaching for a piece of paper folded neatly and pinned to Ramone's sleeve. Since it said "Toby Peters" on it, in what looked like the same pen and block letters as the poem in my pocket, I figured it was for me, unpinned it, and started to unfold it. Something creaked behind me and I shot back through the stall door, throwing my back against the wall next to the dripping sink.

I was breathing hard now, half expecting someone to rush through the toilet door with a big surprise for me. No one came. The battle went on. Sidney screamed "Wow" in the distance and I read the note, wishing that I had brought my duly registered and seldom used .38 with me. Who knew?

"Welcome to the game," the note read. "No time for a proper poem, but cage-e is next. There is more than one way to spell t.h.a.t. And then Lionel Varney."

For a beat or two it made no sense, and then something came through. I recalled the name Varney, the burning of Atlanta. The actor in the Confederate uniform who said he had been beaten out for Rhett Butler.

"Shit," I muttered.

Everyone's a writer, an actor, a producer, a director. I like my jobs straight and simple. No poems or newspaper clips. No riddles or games. You get a threat. I protect. Someone is after you. I find him. You lost your cat or your aunt or your gold fillings, and I'm on the job. I don't do crazies if I can help it. But sometimes you can't help it. I tucked the blood-stained note, the poem, the clipping, and the card into the envelope Gable had given me. It was getting thick and, with the sound of a siren very nearby, it was getting hot.

I got out of the toilet as the police car, from the sound of its siren, pulled up in front of the Mozambique. I could make it though the window in Al Ramone's dressing closet and probably be in my Crosley and on the way home in less than thirty seconds, but Lester knew my name and I was easy to find.

I did go back to Al's dressing room, plucked the photograph of him pretending to be dead and found Varney, or what might have been Varney, in the picture, lying at the far right, beard covering his mouth. I folded the photo into the now-bulging envelope, hurried into the broom closet, where I stood on top of an overturned bucket and stashed the envelope under a carton of Gold Dust Cleanser boxes. It wouldn't be good for me or Gable for the police to find that envelope and what was in it.

I put the bucket in the corner, closed the closet, and moved back onto the stage of the Mozambique, where I was transported back a decade. The place looked bombed. All that was missing was Andy the giant Samoan standing on someone's stomach. Two uniformed cops had sat the sailors down against the bar. Frank, his pal, and their dates or wives were sitting at what was left of their table. Frank spotted me and said, "That's him."

I longed for the bad old days.

"That's him," Lester confirmed.

The two cops looked over at me and I said, "There's a dead baritone in the toilet."

Behind me, the piano player, who had appeared from nowhere, launched into a melancholy version of "After You've Gone."

Chapter 2

Captain G. Lane Price was sitting behind his desk, wearing what looked like the same uniform he had worn a little over ten years ago when he'd shaken my hand, wished me well with my life as a civilian, and gone to lunch with the mayor of Glendale.

Captain G. Lane Price was leaning over to polish his shoes with a spritz from the bottle of Griffin ABC Liquid Black that sat on his desk.

The "G" stood for Gene. Lane Price did not think of himself as a "Gene." At least he hadn't two or three decades ago when he was considering a career in movies, politics, or public relations, whichever came first.

"Pevsner," he grunted, looking up at me for an instant and then returning to the task of shining his shoes. "Don't look much different. A pound here, there. A little gray at the sideburns."

"The scars don't show," I said, standing in the large masculine office complete with leather-covered chairs, a massive desk, and pictures on the walls of dead animals and dead politicians.

"Something to be thankful for. Have a seat."

"And I changed my name to Peters a long time ago, Toby Peters."

"Suit yourself," he said. "Nothing new in the City of Angels."

I sat.

Lane Price was a little more bald, a little more hefty, and a lot darker under the eyes than he had been when I left the Glendale Police Department. Price had always looked like a man who just woke up. Now he looked like a man who wanted to go back to sleep.

"How they look to you?" he said, pulling his chair out from behind the desk so he could show me his shoes.

"Ready for inspection by Patton himself," I said.

"Maybe," he said, pursing his lips and examining his work. "Maybe. But I don't figure the wife and her brother'll be after my shoes. There's plenty to criticize on the way down to keep them occupied." He rolled his chair back behind the desk, tapped his fingers on the clear surface of the desk, and continued, "Last I heard you were doing security at Columbia."

"Warners," I corrected. "Got canned for punching a cowboy star."

"Not Bob Steele?" the chief asked seriously.

"No," I said, to his relief. "I'm a licensed investigator in L.A. County."

"How's the wife? . . ."

"Anne and me," I said, wanting to kick off my tight shoes. "We got divorced when I was at Warners."

"Happens," said Price with a sympathetic shake of the head. "You kill that guy in the Mozambique?"

"No," I said.

G. Lane Price nodded. I wasn't sure what the nod meant. He rubbed the top of his head like Guy Kibbee.

"Somebody killed him," G. Lane went on.

"Looked that way to me," I agreed.

We were getting along just fine so far.

"Two of my men, Frank Oznati and Carmen Harris. They were in the Mozambique with their wives, they say your friend, one who looks like Robert Taylor, started a fight and ran, and you went after Ramone."

"Carmen?" I asked. "There're cops named Carmen now?"

Price shrugged.

"Tends to put a chip on your shoulder," he said. "You went after Ramone. Lou Canton says . . ."

"Lou? . . ."

"Old piano player. Says when he and Ramone left the stage when the fight started, Ramone said he saw someone he knew in the audience. Canton says Al looked scared. Canton helped him to his dressing room and went out to call the station. No phone backstage and he was afraid to go back into the bar."

"Interesting," I said.

"Depends," said Price. "Maybe two, three minutes after you go backstage, you come out and announce that Ramone's dead."

"Right."

"Right," Price said, nodding and pursing his lips. "Questions. Why did you go backstage? What did you see? Who was the guy you were with? And what were you doing in the Mozambique?"

"Which one do you want first?" I asked.

"Take your pick and take your time," the chief said, leaning back and folding his hands behind his head. "Longer we take, the less time I have to spend at my wife's brother's house. Then, after you tell me, you tell it all to Officer Cooper, who takes it down so you can sign."

"I need a lawyer?" I asked.

"This day and age everyone needs a lawyer," Price said, sighing.

"Al Ramone used to be an actor," I said.

"That a fact? Which question you answering?"

"He owed my client a few dollars," I said, turning my most sincere unblinking look at the chief. It was wasted. His eyes were closed.

"A few?" he said, eyes still closed.

"Two hundred and change," I said. "I get forty bucks if I collect from Ramone."

"Client got a name?" Price asked dreamily.

"Everybody's got a name," I said.

"Can I trouble you for it?"

"I don't . . ."

"Just to check if you're on the up-and-up about this," he said, opening one eye to watch my reaction.

"Sheldon Minck," I said. "A dentist in L.A. In the Farraday Building."

"Report says Ramone had a full set of dentures in his lap. What'd he need with a dentist?"

"Old bill," I said.

"This dentist, he doesn't happen to look like, say, some movie star, Robert Taylor maybe?"

Both of Price's eyes were open now.

"Dr. Minck is five-six, about two hundred pounds, bald, and sporting glasses as thick as Yorba Linda."

"Guy who was with you who started the fight . . ." Lane Price went on, checking his watch.

"Don't know anything about him. Just a guy who had a few drinks and was looking for someone to tell his troubles to. He offered me a beer. I took it. He started to tell me the story of his life and wife in Omaha. Then Ramone came out . . . and everything started when the guy from Omaha punched your man and was gone. Ramone left the stage and I went after him."

"Guy from Omaha looked like a movie star," the chief said, sitting up again.

"Maybe," I said. "A little like Edward G. Robinson maybe."

"Not the way I heard it," said the chief.

"Closest star I can give you," I apologized, holding my hands up.

"Backstage. Next scene," said Price. "And slow it down. This is a homicide."

"Looked for Ramone. Couldn't find him. Went into the toilet and there he was."

"That's it?"

"That's it. Didn't see anybody. Didn't hear anything."

The chief started to open his desk drawer, changed his mind, and closed it again.

"Curtain rod from his dressing room," said Price. "Skewered like that Hungarian stuff I hate."

Price demonstrated a two-handed jab with a curtain rod aimed, I guessed, at an imaginary brother-in-law.

"Damn thing doesn't even have a point," he went on. "I mean the curtain rod. Take some strength, don't you know, even if you got lucky and went in right under the ribs, which he did."

"Take some strength," I agreed.

Price stood up and worked the kinks out of his legs.

"Got the knees of an old ballet dancer," he said.

I held back a good comeback with another one in the wings and just nodded. Price had no sense of humor.

"Hell," he said. "I'll buy your story but I'll check it out. Can't see any reason you'd go coconuts on me with a curtain rod for forty bucks. Hell, these are boom times, boom times this side of the Rockies. People don't kill for forty bucks, but you never know."

"You never know," I agreed.

He was standing over me now, looking down, his face sour

with the realization that he'd soon be back with the little woman and her brother.

"Some of what you told me is maybe half true," he said. "I find it's not and you killed Ramone, I'll haul you back to Glendale so fast your ears'll bleed."

"I'm always happy to come back home," I said, "but I didn't . . ."

"Hell," he said with another sigh. "I'm shorthanded here, Peters. You get cleared on this I'll take you back, promotion to sergeant."

I stood up now.

"Damn war's got my good men. Thinking of taking on women for street work," he said to a photograph on the wall of Herbert Hoover.

"I'll think about it," I said as Price walked to his door and opened it.

"No, you won't," he said. "I'm gonna have to make it for the duration with Carmen, Frank, amazons, little kids, and dwarfs."

"Little persons," I corrected.

He looked back at me, puzzled.

"Little persons. They don't like to be called *dwarfs*. My best friend is a little person."

"That a fact?" said Price.

I nodded as he called out the door for Officer Cooper.

"Those sailors didn't start that fight with our cops, and the guy in the booth didn't either," I said as he stepped away from the door, leaving it open. "Your boys started it."

"Figures," said Price, adjusting his suit jacket. "Damn thing is I can't get rid of 'em. They're tough, stupid, and 4-F, one for a trick shoulder and the other for flat feet. Best I can do. When Johnny comes marching home, Frank and Carmen can join the job market. Wait. Now things are coming back to me here. You used to live on . . ."

"Linden," I said. "My dad had a grocery store on Canada."

"You had a brother . . ." he said, squinting at me and trying to remember.

"Phil. He's a cop. Wilshire District. Captain."

"Change his name too?"

"No," I said. "He's still Pevsner."

"Think he'd be interested in a return to his family roots?" asked Price hopefully.

"You can ask," I said as Officer Cooper, lean, teen, and neatly pressed, came in with a notebook in hand.

"How do I look?" asked Price, tugging at his jacket.

"Elegant," I said before Cooper could speak.

"Distinguished," said Cooper seriously.

"Can't trust either of you," Price said. "Take his statement and send him home."

Cooper nodded.

"My car's still at the Mozambique," I said as Price went out the door.

"Cooper," called the chief.

"I'll take him back," said the young cop as the door slammed.

"Doesn't care for his brother-in-law," I said.

"Brother-in-law's the county water commissioner," Cooper was whispering, even though the chief's freshly polished shoes were tapping well down the hallway.

I checked my watch. It told me it was eight-twenty. My watch was wrong as usual. It was the only thing my old man left me besides memories.

"It's five after midnight," Cooper said.

"Let's get to it," I said, sitting again.

Cooper didn't take the chief's chair. He sat opposite me in a chair in front of the desk, balancing the notebook in his lap.

"You know there's more than one way to spell *cagey*," I said.

"Never thought much about it," Cooper said, smoothing his pants and taking out his pencil.

It took about ten minutes to give my statement and another twenty for Cooper to type it up for my signature. I signed and he drove me back to my car in the parking lot of the Mozambique. There was one other car in the lot, an old Ford that glowed with wax or fresh paint by the night light of the Mozambique window.

"Ramone's car?" I asked.

"Wouldn't know," said Cooper.

I got out and went to my Crosley. It wasn't locked. I slid in and started the engine. Cooper just sat there watching me. I pulled out into the street and headed north. When I got to the first corner, I turned right, parked at the curb, turned off the lights, and turned my engine off.

I rolled my window open and thought I heard the sound of Cooper's patrol car pulling out on the dead street behind me. I waited a few minutes, got out of the car, and headed for the Mozambique in the shadows.

The place was dark and the front door was locked. I knocked gently, hoping Lester had had enough for the night and had gone home instead of sitting in the dark on a tinder pile of broken chairs, tables, shot glasses, and beer mugs.

"Wow," Sidney screamed inside.

I waited a few beats, ready with a lie for Lester, Officer Cooper, or an air-raid warden, but I didn't need it. I went to the east side of the Mozambique along the pink adobe wall to the window of Al Ramone's dressing room. It was closed now, but I doubted if anyone had fixed the latch in the last hour. It didn't make much noise as I slid it up and carefully climbed inside.

When I got inside I felt my way past the little dressing table and along the wall to the door. There wasn't much light

from moon, stars, or the all-night ten-watt light bulb somewhere ahead of me through the open door.

I didn't bang my shins or walk into anything as I inched
along the wall and smelled the night dust and alcohol. Across
from the wall, I could make out a dark shadowed area where
the rest room should be. Something? A creak? Sidney? Maybe
Lester let Sidney fly around the Mozambique at night, a guard
cockatoo with beak and claw and limited vocabulary.

Quiet.

I pulled the door of the broom closet open, groped till I
found the bucket, turned it over, balanced myself on it, holding onto the lower shelf. Then I searched for and found the
envelope with Gable's four fifty-dollar bills, his card, the
killer's poem and notes, and the photograph I'd plucked from
Ramone's mirror. I pulled the envelope down and tucked it
into my Windbreaker pocket as I got off the bucket.

I was back in the little alcove, getting used to the ten-watt
light, and was almost inside of Al Ramone's dressing room
when the toilet flushed. I pushed my back against the wall,
trying to cover myself with shadow, knowing I should just
make a break for the window when the rest-room door came
open and the light behind the man in the doorway lit me like
Dame Myra Hess at the Hollywood Bowl.

Chapter 3

"You scared the shit out of me," the old piano player said, his hand on his heart.

"Sorry," I said, stepping away from the wall.

Lou Canton was wearing a ratty bathrobe two sizes too big for him and he was carrying a clear drinking glass with a toothbrush and a can of Dr. Lyon's Tooth Powder in it.

"I'm not a young man," he said. "And with poor Al . . ."

"Sorry," I repeated.

"It's done," he said with a wave of his hand. "Done is done. You came through the window?"

"Yes," I said.

"Told Lester to fix it a month, two months ago," the old man said. "But did he listen? No, he did not listen. Find what you were lookin' for?"

"I wasn't . . . yes," I said.

"Good."

He turned his back on me and headed toward the curtain that led to the bandstand.

"Hold it a second," I said.

Canton, his back to me, slumped and shook his head.

"What? I'm tired. This has been a hell of a day. I'm an old fart and I don't sleep so good at night. What? You don't look like a crazy. I look more like a crazy than you do. So, I don't think you're gonna kill me. Al . . . well, maybe that's another story and you had reasons, but me, I figure it was the other guy. Listen to me, I'm talkin' too much. Happens when you get my age. Nobody listens to you, so you talk to yourself. I don't even listen to me half the time."

"What other guy?" I asked.

"I told Lester," the old man said. "He didn't listen. I told the cops tonight. Did they listen? They didn't listen. Last night. Guy about your height. Thirty, thirty-five. Who knows? Sat at the bar nursing his drink and looking at Al like he was more interesting than Bing Crosby. I'm sorry what happened to Al, but the man had no talent. Couldn't carry a tune. Couldn't remember a bridge. I had to cover for him every time. Ever carry an overweight baritone over a musical bridge? You drop him and you both look bad."

"This guy . . ." I prodded, but Canton, who was rubbing a finger of his free hand across his thin mustache, kept going.

"Guy we're talking about looks like a crazy, maybe. You don't look like a crazy."

"Thanks."

"Not a compliment. The truth. What kind of compliment is it to say a guy doesn't look crazy? How old you figure me for?"

He shook the glass in his hand, tinkling brush and can of tooth powder against the sides.

"Sixty-five, maybe a little more," I guessed.

"Eighty," he said. "I played with Isham Jones. Can you believe that? Did piano and even bass for George Metaxa and Paul Whiteman. Did a Caribbean cruise filling in for Claude Thornhill. No one noticed the difference. And now—" He looked around the alcove and shook his head. "Now, you get old and you sleep on a cot in a bar and talk to a crazy bird."

"The guy at the bar," I reminded him.

"Who knows? Mexican maybe. Or Rumanian. Young more than old. My eyes are good but they're the eyes of a man who has seen a lot. King Oliver said I could read music fifty feet away. With most of those bands, I was the only one could read music even if it was two feet away, if you know what I'm saying to you."

"I know," I said. "About . . ."

". . . the guy at the bar. Dark hair, I think, what was left of it. Getting bald in the front. Jacket like yours, only light-colored. Something written on the pocket. Right here. Something on the pocket. Couldn't read it. Twenty years back, even ten, maybe, I could have, but . . . anyway, Mexican or Rumanian guy, whatever, Al finishes his set, the guy disappears. Came back the next night. Same thing."

"Maybe Lester remembers him," I said.

"Lester," he said with disgust. "My sister's son. Decent guy but no imagination. He thinks I see things where there ain't things. Can I get to sleep now? They're coming in early to clean the place up and fix the furniture."

"Sorry," I said.

"Nothing," he said with a wave, shuffling away, his slippers clapping against the wooden floor.

"You play a hot piano," I said.

"Thanks," he said, moving into darkness. "A little applause never hurts. Turn off the toilet light when you leave. Don't worry. They took Al away about an hour ago."

"Good night."

He disappeared through the curtain leading to the bandstand without another word.

I went out through the window, walked around the corner to my Crosley, and took Canada to South and made my way over to Los Felix on side streets. I hit Highland in about thirty minutes and was up on the porch and inside Mrs.

Plaut's boardinghouse on Heliotrope off of Hollywood Boulevard by two in the morning.

The porch light was off, as they were all up and down the street to thwart the Japanese who might launch kamikaze assaults on rundown Los Angeles neighborhoods in the middle of the night. No one was sure how the Japanese would get close enough to the coast to carry out such an attack, but they had managed a couple of failed attempts from aircraft carriers in the last few years. If the papers were right, the Japanese didn't have anything left to launch a paper plane from, but Lowell Thomas had said on the evening news that they were gathering what was left of their fleet for an attack somewhere. I thought about thousands of Japanese landing in Santa Monica on the beach during a women's volleyball tournament.

I got inside, closed the door gently, slowly behind me and locked it, standing for a beat or two to be sure my landlady, in her rooms to my left, hadn't detected my predawn return. Quiet. Mrs. Plaut had a bird whose name changed as the whim took its owner. But the bird was always covered at night, and while he or she could let out a screech that Butterfly McQueen would envy, he didn't have even a one-word vocabulary.

I took off my shoes and made my way up the stairs, letting experience and instinct guide me past the creaking steps and loose sections of the rickety bannister.

Upper landing and into the bathroom, closing the door behind me before I hit the light switch. Mrs. Plaut had placed heavy red curtains on the small bathroom window. She had sewn a patriotic warning in yellow onto the curtain, one you could not miss whether you were standing, bathing, showering, or sitting. It read: "Flush only when you must. Save paper when e'er you can."

I used the toilet, took off my jacket, and checked on the fifties Clark Gable had given me. Then I washed and shaved

with the razor and remnants of a bar of Palmolive stashed in
the corner of the medicine cabinet.

I was tired. Back in my room across the hall, Dash looked
up at me from the sofa. He blinked once and closed his eyes.

"Hungry?" I said.

He opened his eyes again and considered purring. He was
orange, fat, independent, and well fed. He closed his eyes
again. I took that for a no. Besides, Dash knew better than to
count on me. The window was open and he could do his own
shopping. I owed him for saving my life a year earlier, but I
didn't owe him enough to take away his independence, turn
him into a pet, and make him pretend he liked me.

I took off my clothes, forced myself to hang my jacket and
pants in the closet, dropped my socks and underwear on the
small pile growing in a corner, and, envelope from Gable in
hand, plopped back on the mattress on the floor. I have a bad
back. I can't sleep on a bed. I can't sleep on my stomach. In
addition to the watch, I inherited a championship snore from
my father. I can't sleep in civilized company, but alone and
unobserved I can forget murdered baritones and May Company salesmen, Clark Gable and poems written by a killer
who may or may not be a Mexican or Rumanian.

I took one last look at the notes from Ramone's killer. They
made no more sense to me now than the photograph. I put
everything back in the envelope and shoved it under the edge
of the mattress. I had forgotten to turn off the lights. I looked
around the small room at the ancient overstuffed sofa with the
embroidered pillow that read, "God Bless Us Every One," at
the Beech-Nut Gum wall clock that told me it was almost
three, at the small table near the window with the refrigerator
behind it and the tiny sink nearby. It wasn't much, but it was
paid for till the end of April. The shelves over the sink were
filled with cereal boxes, cans of Spam, tuna, and sardines. The
refrigerator contained bread, milk, a rusting twelve-ounce-size

V-8 (with the suggestion on the label that V-8 would be delicious if poured over my breakfast eggs), a brick of Durkee's Vegetable Oleomargarine, and an assortment of ground A & P coffee. What more could I want?

The lights out.

I forced myself up, careful not to throw my back out, and reached for the switch. The door opened an instant after I hit the switch, and a soft high voice with a German-Swiss accent whispered, "Toby, are you here?"

I turned the light back on and in my boxer shorts greeted Gunther Wherthman.

"Come in," I said.

"No," said Gunther, who wore a blue-velvet robe over pajamas whiter than good vanilla ice cream. "I only wanted to reassure myself that you had returned and were safely ensconced."

"I'm safely ensconced."

Gunther, about a decade younger than me and a foot and a half shorter, plunged his hands into his pockets. His face was as clean shaven and smooth at three in the morning as it was at 8:00 A.M., noon, or midnight. His clear blue-green eyes looked at me and then away. Dash opened his eyes again, looked at Gunther, yawned, and went back to sleep.

"I don't wish to . . ." he began, but I stepped in with, "What's up, Gunther?"

He closed the door and looked up at me.

"Gwen," he said. "She has returned to San Francisco. Sudden. Emergency. She had a call. An old . . . someone she knew before."

It wasn't easy for Gunther, who must have been waiting in his room for hours till I tiptoed in. He had met the young, enthusiastic graduate music-history student when I was on a case in San Francisco. It had been love at second thought, and it had been hard on her. I'd seen them looked at, stared at.

Gwen was no giant, but she wasn't a little person either and she was still a kid.

"She coming back?"

"I do not know," he said. "She will call in a day, perhaps two."

"I'm sorry," I said. I seemed to be saying that a lot tonight, but it had been a long night.

"I appreciate that," he said. "I have been unable to work since she left this morning."

Gunther was a contract translator. He had been many things. A circus performer. An actor in *The Wizard of Oz*. One of my clients. We had become best friends and he had gotten me into Mrs. Plaut's three years earlier. Business had been booming for Gunther since the war. Most of his work came on subcontracts from universities on government contracts to translate documents, newspapers, and magazines from Europe into English for analysis. The universities could handle German, Spanish, French, and Italian, but for Czech, Hungarian, Bulgarian, and Albanian, Gunther was their little man. He worked in his room, which was right next door to mine and about the same size. He woke up every morning, had breakfast in a three-piece suit, and then went back upstairs where he climbed up on the chair in front of his desk to translate.

"I've disturbed you. I can see you are tired."

"A little," I agreed, knowing I couldn't hide it any more than the stomach I was scratching. I would have to hit the Y.M.C.A. over on Hope with more regularity.

He turned and opened the door.

"Breakfast?" I asked. "I've got coffee and Little Colonel's. We can talk then."

"My concerns can wait, but I fear that Mrs. Plaut is expecting us downstairs for something she has prepared," he said solemnly. "I am concerned that she has an agenda."

"Wait," I said, getting the envelope from under my mattress. I took out the poem and handed it, the clipping, the crumpled photograph of Al Ramone as a dead Confederate soldier, and the bloodstained piece of paper about spelling *cage-e* to Gunther, who took them solemnly. The four fifties and the card I shoved in the pocket of my Windbreaker in the closet.

"If you can't sleep, see what you can make of them," I said and then followed up with a thirty-second wrap-up of what had happened in the last seven hours.

When I finished, Gunther simply nodded.

"Good night, Toby," he said.

"Good night, Gunther," I answered.

He backed into the hall, closing the door, and I hit the light switch. Covered by darkness I crawled back onto my mattress on the floor, climbed under my blanket, put my head on the pillow, and went to sleep in no more than the time it took Joe Louis to put Schmeling away in the rematch.

I dreamt of my father holding his wrist up to his ear to listen to the ticking of his watch before he checked the time. My father, dressed in his grocer's apron, smiled, took off the watch, and handed it to me.

I dreamt of Gunther watching Gwen and Clark Gable through a window. Gunther was on my shoulders. Gable and Gwen were on a bed. Then I was on Gunther's shoulders, watching my ex-wife Anne in bed with Clark Gable. With neither Gwen nor Anne did Gable look happy. Then his eyes turned toward Gunther and me watching at the window and he looked disgusted, betrayed.

Dream Three. There are always three with me. Dream Three found Koko the Clown holding one of my hands and Bozo the Dog the other. We were flying through the air over water and Koko kept repeating, "Pretty cagey. Pretty cagey." I thought the dog and the clown were going to drop me. I felt the rush of air under my boxer shorts. I couldn't catch my breath and then I woke up and found daylight flushing the room and Mrs. Plaut standing at the foot of my mattress wearing a blue dress, a white apron, and a very serious look. She was carrying a big yellow bowl in her arms. There is not much of Mrs. Emma Plaut, but what there is is feisty and nearly deaf.

"It's nine," she said.

I tried to sit up. Dash, who had huddled next to my left leg during one of my nightmares, mewed in annoyance and stretched.

"Late breakfast will be at nine-twelve," said Mrs. Plaut.

I grunted something.

"Mr. Gunther is downstairs waiting. Mr. Hill also. And Miss Reynel."

"I know it's pointless," I said. "I know, but something I can't control inside me keeps making me say this. Mrs. Plaut, will you please knock before you enter my room. Please knock and wait till I say 'come in?' "

"Smell this," she said, thrusting the bowl down in front of my nose.

I smelled. It smelled sweet. It smelled comforting.

"Smells good," I said.

"Orange snail muffins," she said, pulling the bowl back. "I will put them on the table in eleven minutes. I expect they will be consumed within a minute after."

"Orange snail muffins?" I asked.

"They contain no snails, if that is your concern," she said. "I believe my Aunt Cora Nathan Wing fed the batter to snails she raised back in Arizona."

"Why? . . ." I began but caught myself. I really did not care why Aunt Cora Nathan Wing raised snails.

"Ten minutes," Mrs. Plaut said, backing out and expertly balancing the heavy bowl in one hand as she closed the door behind her. "And I cannot be responsible for the bad table manners or vicious appetite of Miss Reynel and Mr. Hill."

Dash was out the window and I was out of bed, out of the bathroom, and on the way down the stairs, a pocketful of fifties in my wallet, at eight minutes after, according to the Beech-Nut clock, when the phone rang.

I turned, took the four steps back up, and picked up the hall phone.

"Peters?" came a man's voice, full of enthusiasm and energy.

"Peters," I agreed.

"Sorry about last night," he said.

"Last night? It was a long night with a lot to be sorry for. Give me a hint."

"I left you a note in the Mozambique toilet."

"I got it," I said.

"Figure it out?" he asked brightly.

"I don't like puzzles," I said.

"You can have help on this one," he said. "You must know people who like puzzles."

"I'll work on it."

"Good," he said. "You have almost eight hours."

"I don't do puzzles," I said, "but I've got another trick. I can describe people from their voices."

"Okay, my friend. Give it a try."

"I'm not your friend," I said. "I'm late for orange snail muffins and you killed a pathetic third-rate lounge singer. My friends don't do things like that."

"I'm waiting," said the man. "But I can't wait long. I've got groceries to buy, a letter to write home, and a murder to plan."

"You're about thirty, maybe a little older," I began. "Dark. Hair, what's left of it, combed and brushed back. About average height. Good build and you like to wear a gray windbreaker with something written over or on the pocket."

Silence on the other end of the line.

"How'm I doing?" I asked.

The sound of someone breathing on the other end.

"Can't read what it says on the pocket but I'll figure it out in a day or two," I went on. "I know a fortune teller named Juanita who can give me a hand. Look, I've got to run. Give me a call later or, better yet, give me your phone number and I'll get back to you."

"They killed my father," he said quietly but clearly.

"They?"

"A man of talent, a talented man, a man who could have left his mark on the screen instead of in a dirty ditch."

"Mr. Peelers," Mrs. Plaut screamed from downstairs.

"Hear that?" I said. "If I don't get downstairs, I'll miss the orange snail muffins. You wouldn't want to be responsible for that."

I could smell the muffins. They smelled good.

"Your name's on the list too. You and the movie star," he said bitterly. "But the others go first. After Varney I'll come for you and the king."

"I really would love to stand here all day listening to your threats, but I'm hungry and I haven't had my coffee. Just tell me fast what's going on."

"You know what I look like from my voice. Figure out what I'm doing and why."

He hung up. So did I.

I pulled out my pocket spiral notebook and made some notes with the stub of a pencil I had picked up at No-Neck Arnie the mechanic's. Then I checked the telephone directories on the table next to the phone. No Lionel Varney in greater Los Angeles. I threw a nickel in the phone and pleaded with the information operator to track Varney down. She had five Varneys. No Lionels. I hung up.

"Mr. Peelers," Mrs. Plaut called again, impatiently.

I shuffled to the bathroom, threw water on my face, Jeris hair tonic on my head, and hurried down the stairs. I walked through Mrs. Plaut's living room, where mismatched mementos and oddities from the Plaut family past were neatly laid to rest. A Tiffany lamp with a shade depicting a naked lady on the moon stood next to the sewing chair, a monstrous dull-orange thing of cotton with big arms. A seaman's chest stood under the curtained window facing the front porch. The oriental rug was worn almost to a single tone and only the hint of a design. The rest of the room was restaurant chairs with knitted antimacassars and a bird cage in which the bird was nibbling on seed and gurgling to itself.

In the dining room sat Mrs. Plaut, Gunther, Mr. Hill the mailman, Miss Reynel, a plate in the center of the table on which rested two huge blood-red muffins, and cups filled with coffee.

"You are tardy," Mrs. Plaut said, looking at me with the eyes of my third-grade teacher, Mrs. Eileen Eck.

"Phone call," I said, sitting in the open chair, "sorry."

"Tardy to the party and you miss the ice cream," Mrs. Plaut said, reaching over for my plate and putting a muffin on it.

"I was talking to a murderer," I explained. "He's killed two men. Plans to kill two more before he comes after me and Clark Gable."

This information did not appear to get through to anyone but Miss Reynel, who put down her blue-on-white coffee cup and smiled at my dark but pointless humor. Miss Reynel was a ballroom-dancing instructor at Arthur Murray's. She was recently divorced, pretty of painted face, sultry of red hair, the far side of forty-five, and far too skinny for me to dream about. Mr. Hill, however, looked at the recent addition to our happy home as a vision in the mold of Katharine Hepburn. Mr. Hill spoke of this affliction only with his eyes. Mr. Hill was seldom heard to speak, though at Mrs. Plaut's annual eggnog and family New Year's party he was known to wind up his courage, drink himself into a state which he called happiness, and sing Irish ballads with remarkably little skill.

"Coffee's great," I said, looking down at the muffin.

"Great," echoed Miss Reynel, who was dressed for Monday morning in a don't-touch-me yellow suit with Joan Crawford shoulders.

"Try the muffin," Mrs. Plaut said.

I looked around the table. All but Gunther had, if the crimson crumbs told the truth, consumed at least one of the massive lumps. Gunther's was untouched.

"How are you this morning?" I asked Gunther, pulling the plate a little closer to me.

"Without appetite," he said, gazing at the muffin in front of him, which approximated the size of his head.

"You'll like it," said Mrs. Plaut.

"Why is it red?" I asked.

"You wouldn't want it its natural color," Mrs. Plaut explained as I tore off a piece and started to raise it to my mouth. I took a tentative bite and washed it down with some coffee.

"Not bad," I said.

Mr. Hill smiled. Miss Reynel carefully dabbed the corners of her mouth for crumbs.

"It's supposed to be better than bad," Mrs. Plaut said. "It is supposed to be good."

"It's good," I said.

"Ingredients are difficult to obtain," she said, placing her hands palm-down on the table, ready for business.

"I can appreciate that," I said, taking some more orange snail muffin.

All eyes were on me. I had the feeling I was supposed to say something, but I had no idea what it was.

"We have all agreed, Mr. Peelers," Mrs. Plaut said, "to pool our ration-book resources and comply with the point system which is effective today."

Mrs. Plaut looked around the table for confirmation. She got it from Mr. Hill and Miss Reynel. Gunther was looking at the muffin before him as if it were a ruby crystal ball that would tell him how Gwen and her old boyfriend were getting along in San Francisco.

"The goal of point rationing," Mrs. Plaut said, pouring me more coffee, "is to give us as wide a choice as possible within any group of rationed commodities and to encourage the use of more plentiful foods in preference to the scarcer items."

"Sounds good to me," I said.

"War Ration Book Two will allow each person, including infants, forty-eight points during the first period, for most canned goods and processed soups, vegetables and fruits, and dried beans and peas. More scarce canned foods will require more points."

"Fascinating," I said, working on my muffin.

"The government has urged us to use more fruits and vegetables, spaghetti, and other foods for which no ration stamps are required."

"I see," I said.

"If you did not get your Book Two last week at the school, you can pick it up between three and five Friday. You have to have Book One with you, however. If you lost Book One you have to apply in writing to the ration board. At the time of registering for Book Two you must declare all the coffee you have on hand in excess of one point per person over fourteen years of age when rationing went into effect November 28 of last year. For each excess pound of coffee, one stamp will be taken from Book One. However, Stamp Twenty-five in Book One is good for one pound of coffee through March 21, which means it must last six weeks instead of five, as before. Stamp Eleven in Book One is good for three pounds of sugar through March 15."

"Could you go over that one more time?" I asked, showing my slightly gap-toothed but reasonably Teel-white teeth.

"You are joshing me," Mrs. Plaut said seriously. "A man in your business has little room for levity."

I was not quite sure what business she was referring to. At various times, Mrs. Plaut believed I was an exterminator or a book editor. I was and had been editing Mrs. P.'s family memoirs for over a year, chapter by chapter as she completed them.

"You are right," I said.

"As I see it, you have an obligation to contribute."

"You can have half my food-ration stamps," I said. "I'm keeping my A, B, and C unit coupons for gas and tires."

"Period Four Coupons," Mrs. Plaut parried.

"Period Four?" I asked, backing up.

"Fuel oil," she said triumphantly.

"They're yours."

She sat back and looked at her boarders; the conquering hero.

"It's been a long war," I said.

"Particularly hard on a sweet tooth," Mrs. Plaut said with a sigh. "More coffee? Another muffin?"

Sweet tooth. I'd forgotten Shelly Minck. I looked at my watch, which told me it was eight. I refused its sprung lies and asked Gunther the time. Without taking his eyes from the muffin, he pulled out his pocket watch and turned it to me. Ten.

" 'Scuse me," I said, getting up and moving fast toward the door.

"Don't forget," Mrs. Plaut said. "The book."

"I won't," I said, not knowing whether she meant the chapter of her book I was supposed to be reading or the ration book she had wheedled out of me.

I went up the stairs fast in spite of the fact that going upstairs fast has thrown my back out six times. As I ran, I pulled a nickel from my pocket and was reaching for the coin slot on the upstairs pay phone while I was still moving. I dialed Shelly's and my office. The phone rang. I let it ring. A dozen times. No answer. Maybe good. If I couldn't reach him, maybe Chief G. Lane Price of the Glendale Police couldn't either. I hung the phone up and started down the stairs. Gunther stood at the bottom looking up.

"I've thought about this *ca-gee*," he said. "The one in the note you gave me."

I stopped when I got to the bottom and looked at him expectantly.

"It could be the Hungarian word for bad spring wine," he said.

"Doesn't fit," I said, walking toward the front door with Gunther at my side.

"*Kah-Chee,*" he tried. "The Nepalese chant of extreme contrition."

"Not likely," I said, opening the door. The sun was shining.

"Then simply *cagey*," Gunther went on. "The American slang word for protectively cautious and clever."

"Don't think so, Gunther," I said, stepping out.

"Without knowing how it is spelled, it is difficult to pursue."

"I appreciate that," I said, pulling out my car key.

"The most likely solution, however," Gunther said, "is that *K.G.* are initials, initials of the next victim."

"That one I like," I said. "Keep at it."

"I shall," he said as I hurried down the cement path to the curb where my Crosley was parked.

I got in, started the engine, and waved at Gunther, who was standing solemnly under the photograph of Eleanor Roosevelt nailed to the white wood behind him. Mrs. Plaut thought it was Marie Dressler.

Chapter 4

The Farraday Building is downtown, just off of Ninth Street on Hoover. Parking on the street is a game of chance. The other options aren't much better. No-Neck Arnie's three blocks away, where I'd have to pay half a buck each in and out, or the alleyway behind the Farraday, where derelicts were known to nest, demand tribute and ignore the sacred trust of watching my Crosley.

I found a magical space on the street. Right in front of Manny's taco shop. An omen or a setup for disappointment?

No one was in the lobby which, as always, smelled scrubbed and antiseptic thanks to the efforts of the landlord, Jeremy Butler—poet, former professional wrestler, and, at the age of sixty-three, recent husband and father. The Farraday was his legacy for his wife, Alice, and his infant daughter, Natasha. The bald giant had vowed to keep it free of vagrants, vermin, and mildew.

According to Jeremy, who knew about such things, the Farraday was on the site of the last battle of the Mexican War in 1848. The two-year battle with Spain over who owned California had ended with a rebellion not by the Spanish army but Californios, the descendants of the original Spanish settlers going back to the 1500s. In August of 1848, after the United

States had formally defeated Mexico, the U.S. military commander in Los Angeles, Lieutenant Archibald Gillespie, gave the defeated Californios a list of rules about how they were to behave under the new flag. The Californios, who had never considered themselves particularly Mexican and didn't find the U.S. Army or its underranked commander in California particularly civilized, put together a rebellion of ranch workers, land owners, and townspeople among the four thousand men, women, and children who lived in Los Angeles. Under the leadership of Andres Pico, brother of the colorfully named governor of Lower California, Pio Pico, the volunteer band did what the Spanish had been unable to do. They threw the American army out of Los Angeles. Gillespie returned. The Californios threw him out once more. It was this second battle which Jeremy claimed was fought on the site of the Farraday Building.

When Gillespie returned the next time, a month later, with more troops and the title of Military Commander of the South, the Californios were seriously outmatched and they surrendered at Campo La Cienega. Now, almost a hundred years later, the descendants of the Californios, and those who claimed they were, had still not forgiven the U.S. and its army.

I opened the lobby door and stepped into the broad open inner lobby that reached six stories high, with offices on each level. There was an elevator, an ancient, open cage, but I was in a hurry. I climbed, baby-talking my back, asking it to be calm and reasonable.

There was a skylight, small dark panes of glass in the ceiling six stories above the open tiled lobby. The sunlight and dim landing bulbs were enough to light my way past tiers of baby photographers, fortune tellers, talent agencies, importers of who-knows-what, costume jewelers, and publishers of pornography. I was the only private investigator. Sheldon

Minck, D.D.S., Master of Dental Hygiene, was the only dentist. We shared an office on the fifth floor.

No, we didn't share an office. Shelly had the office. I sublet a closet with the window overlooking the alley. My office wasn't much larger than the dressing room of the late Al Ramone.

The outer-office door was open. I went in. The lights were on. Bad sign. Shelly was here. Price had probably talked to him. The tiny waiting room was relatively clean, the magazines—*Life, Colliers, Woman's Day,* and *Look*—were piled on the small table in front of the three chairs.

I went through the inner door and found Sheldon Minck sleeping in his dental chair, his arms folded over one of his magazines, his stained white smock bunched under his neck. His thick glasses had slipped perilously toward the end of his nose and his cigar looked like a dark springboard, bouncing with each breath. Shelly must have sensed my presence. He dropped the magazine and swatted the top of his head.

"Ugg," he cried, staggering forward out of the chair, opening his eyes, swinging at some real or imagined insect with his fluttering magazine. He tottered back into my arms.

"You were dreaming, Shel," I said, straightening him up.

"Wha?"

"Dreaming," I repeated, turning him around to face me.

I straightened his smock, marveling at his ability to keep his glasses on his nose and cigar in his teeth while in full flight from a nightmare.

"Toby," he said.

"Yes, Shel."

He took the cigar from his mouth and said, "Publishing."

"Publishing, Shel?"

"Came to me in the dream," he said, slapping the magazine and moving to the sink, where he turned on the cold-water tap, cupped his hand, and took a drink.

"A dream?"

"Yeah," he said, turning back to me, a trickle of water on his chin, his cigar back in his mouth. *Tooth Talk*, a magazine, and here's the beauty part, for patients, people who have something wrong with their teeth. Everybody's got something wrong with their teeth. We'll have articles on celebrities with great teeth. Who's got great teeth?"

"Lassie," I said.

"Joking," he said, returning to his dental chair, "but why not? Keeping the teeth of movie animals clean and cavity-free. Great article. Short stories about teeth. Poetry about teeth. Ads, we'll fill it with ads."

Shelly's eyes, huge behind the thick glasses, got even wider in anticipation of the ad revenue.

"Coloring your teeth, a new beauty concept," he said, looking up at the ceiling. "Remember my idea about that?"

"Vividly," I said.

"Dentists who wanted to write would have a place to send their ideas, their creative work. Even, why not, drawings, paintings. By dentists, for dentists."

Shelly was out of his chair now, shaking his head as new ideas sprang from whatever he had eaten for breakfast.

"Sounds like a good idea to me, Shel," I said.

"Yeah," he said with a grin. "How about this? Special section at the end of each issue for kids. Cartoon. Jimmy Chew versus Sammy Grinder. Jimmy's a handsome white incisor who takes care of himself. Sammy Grinder is covered in buildup, maybe even has a kind of five-o'clock shadow. Ideas like this. Start small. Work it up. Maybe get a few of those movie clients of yours to invest."

"Worth a try," I said.

"Yeah," he said, dreamily rubbing his palms together as if he were trying to start a fire.

Then he stopped suddenly and a new look appeared as he turned his head to me.

"You've never agreed with any idea I've ever had."

"This is an exception," I answered. "It's so . . ."

"You want something," he said, advancing on me, a roly-poly ball of white-smocked suspicion. "What?"

"Small favor," I admitted.

"Small?" He was a foot away now, a good eighteen inches closer than I wanted him. "Ah," he said.

"You hired me on a contingency basis to collect a bill for dental work from a guy named Al Ramone," I said, walking to the sink, turning on the water, and ignoring the pile of grimy coffee cups and dental surgery instruments. I washed my face, my back to Sheldon Minck, and shook myself almost dry.

"I did not," Shelly said.

I turned to face him. He was watching my eyes to see where all this was going and how much he could get out of it.

"You did. Mr. Ramone has met an untimely death," I explained.

"Tell me a timely one," Shelly fought back.

"I'd rather not. I need a favor, Shel," I continued. "Someone asks you, you hired me to get your payment. Al Ramone. Okay?"

"Can't be done," Shelly said, removing the cigar from his face and looking down at it as if it were some vile wet thing, which it was.

"I think your dental magazine is a great idea," I tried.

"No, you don't, Toby," he said.

"I think it's one of your best ideas," I said.

He looked at me again. "Can't be done," he repeated.

"What, the dental magazine or the favor?"

"Favor," he said. "Guy named Price already called. Asked if

you were working for me, asked if I was interested in becoming a Glendale policeman."

"And you told him? . . ."

"You weren't doing any work for me. I'm a dentist and not interested in a career change."

I started toward my office.

"You're in trouble?"

I shrugged. He followed me.

"You shouldn't tell lies," he said behind me.

"Shelly, you tell more lies than Tojo."

"Well, yes, maybe, but that doesn't make it right."

I went into my office, a cubbyhole with a door, a box big enough for a small desk with a chair behind it, two small chairs in front of it. Behind the desk chair was a window, six floors above the alley. On the wall across from the desk, next to the door, was a framed photograph of my father, me, my brother Phil, and our dog Kaiser Wilhelm. I was about ten when the picture was taken. Phil was fourteen or fifteen. Our father was wearing his grocer's apron and the look of a man smiling through pain. Kaiser Wilhelm was expressionless. On the wall to our right as we came in was a painting that covered the entire available space, the painting of a woman cradling two identical children on her lap. The painting had been done by Salvador Dali.

"You should have called," Shelly said, closing the door behind him as I moved behind the desk and sat.

"I did," I said, looking at the top envelope of my morning mail. "You weren't here."

"How was I to know?"

"You weren't," I said. "Now, if you'll leave me alone, I've got a suicide note to write."

Shelly leaned over the desk at me.

"I'm for chrissake sorry, Toby," he said.

"You're for chrissake forgiven, Sheldon," I said.

"Does this mean you think my magazine idea stinks?"

"No," I said. "It's better than your Bernie the Bicuspid children's book."

"Tony the Tooth. Tony the Tooth," he corrected, shaking his head. "That was a good idea, Toby. A great idea whose time hasn't come. That's why I want to ease it into the new magazine. The grinder and incisor."

The outer door to the dental office opened and closed behind Shelly. He turned as someone walked in.

"New patient," he whispered, turning back. "Ten o'clock. Almost forgot."

He walked out, closing the door behind him.

I worked on a new lie while I opened my mail.

The first letter was from the Barbizon-Plaza Hotel in New York City. I'd stayed there on a case. The Barbizon told me it was famous for its continental breakfast, which came with rooms as low as three bucks a day. All rooms with private baths and radios.

I could tell Price that Shelly was lying. That he was afraid of bad publicity.

The second letter was from the San Diego Book Club, promising me a choice of I Saw the Fall of the Philippines, by Carlos P. Romulo, or Congo Song, by Stuart Cloete, for a nickel.

I could deny I had told Price anything. I'd never be able to return to Glendale, but there are worse exiles.

The last of my mail was a postcard with a map on the front that told me how to get to the Old Hickory Barbecue off of Echo Park Avenue. Two free parking lots. Open all night. Two minutes from downtown. There wasn't much room for the message on the front because the preprinted P.S. filled the bottom half with a message that the Old Hickory was the most unusual eating place in America.

"The first dead soldier is now really dead," the note said.

"And the cage-e one is next. I began lame but I'll end able. Who am I? Just ask what I am d.o.i.n.g." It wasn't signed.

There was no stamp on the postcard. It hadn't come through the mail. I took the poem and the bloody note from my pocket, cleared a space on the table, and laid them crumpled and flat in front of me. They made no more sense than they had last night.

I got up, went to the door, opened it, and watched Shelly flashing a silver pocket flashlight into the mouth of a young man covered with a gray-white sheet. Sheldon Minck was singing "Straighten Up and Fly Right."

"Shel," I said. "When did you get the mail?"

"Usual time," Sheldon said, pausing in his song but not his work. "About eight."

"Downstairs?" I said, looking at the young man in the chair.

"Hold still, Mr. Spelling," Shelly said to his patient. "The best is yet to be. Downstairs."

"Thank you."

"Cool down, papa, don't you blow your top," Shelly sang, poking Mr. Spelling's teeth with something that looked like a chopstick with a needle at its tip.

Mr. Spelling grunted in what might have been pain or an urgent desire to plead for mercy.

"Won't take long. Won't take long," Shelly said, probing. "You want 'em clean, I've got to dig. Law of the dental jungle. Safari into the darkest cavities."

Mr. Spelling grunted and I returned to my desk and the poems as Shelly began to question his patient about his potential interest in a magazine devoted to teeth.

> They die until you understand
> They die by weapons in my hand.
> My father wept to be so cut

> From fortune, fame deservéd, but
> I'll avenge the wrongs and slight
> To be there e'er the Ides and right
> Those wrongs and claim his prize
> And give to you a great surprise.
> First there was Charles Larkin
> And next Al Ramone. Do harken
> For on it goes and blood be thine
> Unless you learn to read my s.i.g.n.

It made no more sense this time than it had the night before. I looked at the note that had been pinned to Al Ramone:

"Welcome to the game. No time for a proper poem, but cage-e is next. There is more than one way to spell t.h.a.t. And then Lionel Varney."

I turned the notes and the postcard over, held them up to the window, wondered if I was hungry enough to take a break after a full five minutes of work. I didn't have to decide. My office door opened and Jeremy Butler entered when I called "Come in."

Six-three and three hundred pounds of Jeremy filled my office door. He was wearing dark slacks and a blue pullover sweater with long sleeves and a turtleneck collar. He looked more like the wrestler he had been than the sixty-three-year-old landlord who writes poetry.

"Just the man I want to see," I said, getting up.

"Two policemen were here early this morning looking for you," Jeremy said. "They asked me to tell you to see your brother as soon as you got in."

"They said my *brother*?"

"They said Captain Pevsner and left no address. I assumed they knew he was your brother."

"Why?"

"Why did I assume?" Jeremy raised his voice over the

sound of Shelly's dental machine, set to chip away plaque and enamel. "Because they did not wait for you, though I said you would probably be in shortly."

"Thanks," I said. "Do me a favor, Jeremy. Look at these."

I turned the poem, card, and message toward him.

"May I sit?" he asked.

"Please."

He sat, removed a pair of half glasses from his pocket, put them on, and read.

"She's making lots of dough, working for Kokomo," Shelly belted out beyond the closed door.

Jeremy read slowly and then read a second time.

"The ides is the fifteenth of the month," said Jeremy, looking up and removing his glasses. "The ides of March was the day that Julius Caesar was assassinated. He was told to beware the ides of March, but he did not heed the warning."

"What about the ides of February?"

"No significance that I am aware of," he said. "Who are Charles Larkin and Al Ramone? And Lionel Varney?"

"The first two are dead. Murdered by our poet. I don't know about Varney. I think they were all extras in *Gone With the Wind*," I said. And then I told Jeremy what had happened last night, including my meeting with Clark Gable and Captain Price.

"I see," said Jeremy, putting his glasses back on and looking again.

"I've got a nut here, Jeremy," I said, trying to ignore Shelly's attempt to simulate the sound of a riveting machine as he sang "Rosie the Riveter."

"A nut who likes to play with words," he said. "I like to play with words. If I may copy . . ."

"Take them, keep them safe, work on them," I said. "With my gratitude and blessing."

Jeremy took the material and placed it gently into his

pocket. He nodded. "You see that each of his messages ends with a word broken into letters. S.i.g.n. T.h.a.t. D.o.i.n.g."

"I see," I said, seeing but not understanding.

"He wants to be caught, Toby," Jeremy said. "He leaves puzzles. Tells too much. Taunts. Challenges. This is a man to be wary of. Urges you to follow, leaving small crumbs on the trail. At the end of the trail, you may well find that he has lured you deeply into the woods."

"I'll be careful, Jeremy. Thanks."

Jeremy rose and so did I. I had done a good ten-minute office day and I had work to do. I'd see Captain Phil Pevsner after I'd gotten more answers from my client.

"One more thing," Jeremy said, pausing in the door. "Your murderer is willing to make too many sacrifices. Meter, rhyme, and the proper word give way to his passion to perpetrate the puzzle, to perplex. He has no real interest in poetry."

"Sorry to hear that, Jeremy," I said as Jeremy stepped into Shelly's office. I followed, closing the door behind me.

"Almost done," Shelly said to his patient. "Keep the mouth open wide."

He stepped back, retrieved his cigar from the nearby stand, put it in his mouth, and examined his handiwork. The young man in the chair had closed his eyes. His mouth was dutifully wide.

"I'll show these to Alice," Jeremy said, tapping the clues in his pocket. "She has a beautiful sensitivity to the written word."

Alice Pallis had been a pornography publisher in the Farraday before she heard the muse and married Jeremy. Alice's primary qualification as a pornography publisher had been her ability to pick up the two-hundred-pound printing press and escape with it out the window when the cops came. For almost two years now, Alice had turned her interests to her husband, child, and the publishing of poetry.

"Thanks, Jeremy," I said.

He left and I turned to Sheldon, who was back in his patient's mouth.

"Good teeth," he was telling the victim. "An energetic cleaning was all you needed."

I went back into my office and made two phone calls. The first was to Mame Stoltz at M-G-M. She answered after the fifth ring with "Stoltz, Publicity."

"Peters, Trouble," I said.

"I'm busy, Peters Trouble," she said in her hoarse efficient voice.

"I'll make it fast."

"We've got interviews lined up on *Madame Curie*," she said, sighing. "I'm not gonna tell you how much we're sinking into publicity on this one, but I'll give you a hint. You could probably find a cure for measles with what we've got budgeted."

"You know Gunther Wherthman?" I asked.

"Composer, R.K.O.?" she asked, and I could tell that she was leaning back to light a Camel.

"No, munchkin from *The Wizard of Oz*. Friend of mine. Working with me on a case. Mind if he comes over and looks through the *Gone With the Wind* records?"

"That's Selznick stuff," she said. "We store some of it over in—"

"I'm talking about payroll lists. And a security report. Night of Saturday, December 10, 1938. Maybe accidental death of an extra."

"Atlanta burning," she said immediately. "We've got payroll and I'll see what I can do about security records, but I don't remember anybody getting killed that night . . . what's going on?"

"Dinner on me. Saturday. Sunday. Even Friday."

I'm no beauty, but I knew that Mame had a hard spot in her anatomy for mush-nosed cops, present and former. She had

gone with a sergeant named Rashkow out of the Wilshire before he got drafted. Mame was no beauty, but she had something that could pass for class. She was too skinny for my
taste, an efficiency copy of Ida Lupino with too much makeup.
She did have a pouty mouth like Lupino, but there was nothing soft about Mame. I like soft. I also like doing what I get
paid for, and Mame knew more about M-G-M and Selznick
International than Mayer himself.

"I'll make dinner," she said. "Saturday. You know how to
get to my place?"

"I remember," I said, recalling clearly my escape from
Mame's little cottage in Culver City a year or so ago.

"Send the little man," she said. "I'll see what I can do."

I outlined what I needed for her and she listened, probably
taking notes.

"When you have something, call me at this number," I
said, giving her Clark Gable's phone.

"I know that number, Toby," she said. "I've called it hundreds of times. What are you up to?"

"Making a living," I said. "Mame, go along with me on
this, please."

"You've been keeping up at the Y.M.C.A.?" she asked in a
whisper.

"When I can," I said.

"We'll see Saturday," Mame said.

And she hung up. I called Gunther and asked him to get
over to M-G-M to see Mame as fast as he could, to get his
hands on whatever he could find about the dead extra, and to
track down Lionel Varney. He agreed and I hung up.

"I'm leaving, Shel," I said, going back into the outer office.

He didn't answer.

"I'll call in or be back."

"Right," he said over his shoulder. "Where you goin'?"

"To see the king," I said.

Chapter 6

Sunset to Beverly Glen and west along 101 following the Los Angeles River into the wilderness of Encino. It took almost an hour and I got a headache from the hot wind blowing from the east through the open window and the bad news on the radio from Raymond Gram Swing. The Japanese Army was digging into the Pacific Islands, burrowing tunnels, making the troops pay with ten lives an acre for places called Rabaul, Mindanao, Leyte, and Guam, places we didn't want in the first place. We were winning land and the war and losing lives.

I found a gas station, Jimmy Kelly's Gas and Sundries, specializing in Sinclair products and customer disdain. I used up my ration stamps for the week and bought a Pepsi and a small bottle of Bayer aspirin. I threw a handful of aspirin in my mouth and washed it down with Pepsi while the kid attendant shook his head and avoided my eyes.

When I left the station, I wasn't sure if I was on my way to losing the headache or was so full of aspirin that the question wasn't relevant.

Gable's directions to the ranch were fine and I pulled up in front of the modest white-brick two-story house just before noon. I got out of the Crosley and rang the front door bell. No answer. Something hummed far away behind the house. I rang again and then knocked. Nothing.

I looked through the curtained downstairs windows but the sun didn't help the view. So, I walked behind the house and found myself on a stone patio, looking down a slope toward a copse of grapefruit trees on the left and a white wooden stable on the right. The stable looked empty and the trees looked heavy with overripe fruit.

There didn't seem to be a swimming pool.

I knocked at the back door. No answer.

The metallic rumble beyond the stable grew louder. I turned and watched as a motorcycle burst through the trees along a dirt path and shot toward me.

I stood motionless as it buzz-sawed forward at about sixty miles an hour, shot over a small ridge and took off into the air, hit the grass, and screeched to a halt about ten feet in front of me. Gable, dressed in dark slacks and a short-sleeved yellow pullover shirt, his hair wild, turned off the engine, kicked down the stand, got off the bike, and pulled a small rifle from the tooled-leather holster tied to the bike.

"Don't move," said Gable, cocking the rifle and aiming it at me.

"Look," I began, and took a step forward.

Gable raised his rifle and fired. The bullet whined past my left leg and I hopped away from it.

"Hey," I shouted. "It's me, Peters. I work for you, remember?"

Gable dropped the barrel of the rifle and smiled.

"That's one reason I want you alive," he said. "Look."

I looked where he was pointing, just behind me. On the stone patio, about three feet away, a headless rattlesnake was writhing.

"Hot weather brings 'em out," said Gable, rubbing his unruly hair back. "Sun themselves on the stone. You almost stepped on him."

"Thanks," I said.

"Let's go inside," he said, walking past me. "I'll get rid of our friend later."

He went to the back door, opened it with a key on a small ring, and went inside. I followed into a huge kitchen.

"Sandwiches in the refrigerator. Made them this morning. Beer, whatever. Help yourself."

He pointed toward a steel door in the corner.

"Be right back," he said. "Set up whatever you find in the dining room, through that door."

I crossed the kitchen and opened the door to a walk-in refrigerator. I found a plate of sandwiches, cucumber, onion, ham with butter. White bread. There was plenty of beer. I went for a row of Pepsis at the rear of a shelf about eye level. I juggled the food past a kitchen table covered with a white oil-cloth decorated with little red flowers, pushed through a double door, and placed the food on the dining-room table. I opened the Pepsi with an opener on my pocket knife and looked around.

The room was dark and big, with an open bar on one wall and a whitewashed brick fireplace on another. The walls were dark wood, as was the polished floor. There was an oval rug under the wooden table and another smaller rug under a round game table in the corner. The chairs were wood, no cushions. This was a man's room except for the built-in cabinets on the walls filled with pink plates. A chandelier over the large table was made of old oil lamps.

"Find what you need?" asked Gable, coming in with the rifle under one arm and a dark wooden box under the other.

I pointed at the food and he sat down across from me, laid down the rifle, and opened the box.

Over the sandwiches I told him what had happened the

night before, after he had left the Mozambique. I also told him about Gunther and Mame.

"I know her," he said. "Skinny. Tough. Holds her own."

"That's Mame," I said. "We just wait here and . . ."

"I want you to tell the police that I hired you," he said, chewing on a mouthful of ham sandwich.

"If I have to," I said.

"You won't do me a hell of a lot of good in jail," Gable said. "Thanks."

"So," he said, "we just sit here and wait till your friend and Mame find Cay-gee and Varney, if they do, and hope your poet pal figures out what the lunatic notes from a murderer might mean?"

"We can take a quick tour of the house," I said.

He cocked his head to one side and gave me a lopsided grin.

"You curious, or . . ."

"This is an easy house to get into," I said. "Maybe I'm a little curious."

"Suit yourself," Gable said, standing and picking up his rifle.

We moved to the south wall and he opened sliding doors and led me into the living room.

In contrast to the Irish-tavern feel of the dining room, the living room was warm and sunny, with wall-to-wall yellow-wool carpeting. Two big yellow sofas faced each other, with two green chairs flanking them, and a pair of identical upholstered red armchairs looking on. There were tables along the wall—wood, dark. The drapes were white and green with red flowers. Four large windows let in the light and looked out onto the front lawn. Across from the windows was an old cabinet, filled with a collection of china pitchers.

"This way," Gable said, moving past a high-mantled fireplace to a door he pushed open.

We stepped into Gable's gun room; one wall, maybe thirty feet long, was lined with rifles.

"Expecting an attack on Encino?" I asked.

"Not if I can help it," he said soberly, putting the rifle he had been holding into a rack.

There were lounge chairs and built-in couches in the room but no signs of unwelcome guests.

We marched through a powder room, a maid's room, and an office with yellow walls before making our way upstairs. Two bedrooms, no guest room.

"My suite," he said, pointing through an open door.

The carpet was clean and white.

The first room was brown and beige; the centerpiece was a double bed with a brown-leather headboard. The second room was a kind of study with a small bar and built-in bookcases.

"Desks against the wall," he said, pointing. "Antique, pine, a gift from Selznick, prop from *Gone With the Wind*."

The beige-marble bathroom was pretty fancy but it had no tub, just a shower in one corner.

We left the suite and when we stepped into the corridor, he pointed to a door and said with a sigh "Ma's suite."

He opened the door for me but didn't follow me inside Carole Lombard's bedroom. The room looked as if it had just been cleaned. It had the same carpeting as that in Gable's suite, but that's where the similarity ended. Her bed was a four-poster with a billowy cover. There were white throw rugs on the floor, and near the window stood a full-sized harp. The bathroom and mirrored dressing room were white marble with white fur on the floor and a crystal chandelier on the ceiling.

"House looks clean," I said, coming back into the corridor. Gable nodded and started down the stairs.

He led me back to the gun room, where he picked up the rifle he had recently fired, found some oil and rags and a cleaning box, and sat.

"Used to be filled with life," he said. "Stray cats, dogs. People. You're sitting in Fred MacMurray's favorite chair. Man knew how to laugh. I wonder if he still does."

I kept my mouth shut.

"What now?" he said.

"We could listen to the radio," I suggested, nodding at a tabletop Philco.

He got up, turned it on, and we listened to "Big Sister" and "The Goldbergs." Solomon Goldberg was planning to join the army and Molly was taking the news with pathos and patriotism.

Gable didn't seem to listen. He was lost in getting the rifle as shiny as his spit-polished shoes.

"You married, Peters?" Gable asked finally as he closed his cleaning box.

"Not now," I said.

He nodded knowingly.

"Your fault? Hers? Nobody's?"

"Mine," I said. "Anne wanted me to grow up. I didn't want to."

"What happened to her?"

"Married again. Lost her husband. I keep trying to convince her that I can act my age, but she won't buy it."

"Should she?"

"No," I said.

"Had one happy year here, Peters," Gable said, looking around the gun room. "And then . . ."

The phone rang.

It was in the corner on an area table near the door. Gable walked over and picked it up on the third ring.

"Yes . . . who is this? . . . no, we haven't figured . . . how did you get this number?"

I was out of my chair and standing in front of Gable, whose eyes met mine.

"Him?" I mouthed.

Gable confirmed with a nod as he listened. I held out my hand for the phone. Gable handed it to me.

". . . your idea that she fly, your idea that she go across the country selling stamps and bonds. You killed your own wife as surely as you killed . . . are you listening, hero?"

"I'm listening," I said.

"Peters. I want Gable back."

Gable stood, hands at his sides, serious eyes searching my face.

"Why?"

"Because I want him to suffer the way he made my father suffer before he died."

"I hate to repeat myself here but why do you want him to suffer? What do you think he did?"

"Killed my father," the man said. "Took away his only chance at recognition. He'll pay, Peters. And so will you and everyone who was there when . . ."

"When? . . ."

"What you want to know doesn't mean crap to me, Peters. Since you're out in Encino, I guess you haven't figured out my directions to the next victim."

"I'm working on it," I said.

"I'm going to hang up now, and go kill K.G. You aren't too bright, Peters."

"No," I admitted. "But I don't give up. I never give up. So, hang up, don't hang up, call again, or keep your mouth shut. Sometime I'll tap you on the shoulder and make a hole in your face when you turn around."

"Good-bye, Peters," he said and broke the connection.

I handed the phone to Gable, who hung it up.

"You know what I think," said Gable, folding his arms. "I think he's a fan of my dead wife, that he blames me for her death and . . ."

"He said you killed his father," I interrupted.

"His father? Who the hell is his father?"

I shrugged and the phone rang again. This time I picked it up.

"Yes," I said.

"Toby," said Gunther. "There are seven people with the initials K.G. who worked on *Gone With the Wind* in some capacity. Miss Stoltz has been very helpful in tracking them down quickly. Two of the people are now in the armed services, stationed in the South Pacific. Three are definitely out of the state of California. One is working in a play now in Cleveland. Another is in New York City. The fifth is a Negro woman named Kate Greenway who seems to be impossible to find, though word has it that she has returned to her family in Mississippi. This leaves Karen Gilmore, an extra, and Karl Albert Gouda, also an extra."

"You know where these people are, Gilmore and Gouda?"

"I have addresses and phone numbers for both," Gunther said.

I pulled out my notebook and took the information.

"On the other question, I am afraid I have found little. Lionel Varney was on the payroll. No home address. Access to security files for Selznick International was made possible by Miss Stoltz. But there appears to be no record of the mishap in 1938. It seems there was a fire . . ."

"And security records were destroyed. Good work, Gunther," I said.

"Miss Stoltz is a remarkable woman," Gunther said.

"You can go home now, Gunther. Thanks."

"I made a complimentary remark concerning Miss Stoltz," Gunther said.

"I heard."

"I would like to take the liberty of inviting Miss Stoltz to dinner," he said.

"Invite away," I said as Gable grew clearly impatient.

"I have a sense, however, that she harbors certain feelings, expectations related to you," he said.

"Steal her from me, Gunther. With my blessing."

"You don't think it would be disloyal to Gwen if I simply . . ."

"No," I said. "I've got to try to prevent a murder, Gunther."

"I'm sorry," he said sincerely.

I said good-bye and hung up.

"Two possibles," I said to Gable, placing another call as I laid my open notebook in front of me on the table.

"I'll take one of them," Gable said, holding out his hand. "You can't be in two places at once."

I held up a finger as Alice Pallis answered on the second ring.

"Toby," I said. "Is Jeremy there?"

"It's creation time," Alice said seriously.

Creation time took place in the afternoon. Jeremy sat quietly for about two hours waiting to be kicked in the imagination by a muse. She showed up about once a week to torture him.

"Okay," I said. "When creation time is over, will you ask him to come to this address."

I gave her Gable's address in Encino.

"And what does he do when he gets there?" Alice asked.

"He keeps Clark Gable from getting hurt," I said.

There was a long silence on Alice's end. In the background I could hear Natasha, her baby, cooing at something.

"He is not a young man, Toby. We've talked about this."

"Last time, Alice. I promise."

"I don't believe you, Toby," she said. "But . . . it's really Clark Gable?"

I held out the phone for Gable.

"I don't need a bodyguard," he said. "I don't want a bodyguard. I won't have a bodyguard."

"The man needs a sense of self-worth," I said. "He's a fan. Humor me."

Gable shrugged and took the phone.

"Madame," he said. "This is Clark Gable. I would very much appreciate your husband's help for a brief period. I'm confident that there is no danger here."

Gable was silent for an instant and then closed his eyes.

"I love you Scarlett and by heaven you're going to learn to love me," he said and then listened to Alice for an instant before adding, "You're welcome. Good-bye."

He hung up the phone and looked at it for a beat or two before turning to me again.

"I hope you know what you're doing," he said.

"Trust me," I said, and then I called the Wilshire police station in Los Angeles and talked to Captain Phil Pevsner, my brother. After that I called Selznick International and asked for Wally Hospodar. Wally, I was told, had retired and lived in Calabasas. The man who took my call gave me Wally's phone number when I convinced him Wally and I were old friends. I hung up and tried Wally's number. A woman answered after five rings. I told her I was looking for Wally. She said she'd get the message to him if he called and he'd probably call back.

When I finished the call, Gable showed me the way out of the house. "I don't like just sitting here, Peters," he said, opening the front door for me.

"I'll call," I said. "I promise. Second I know anything. I'll call."

"Oh, the hell with it," he said with a sigh and closed the door on my back.

By breaking speed laws in Van Nuys and Beverly Hills, I got to the address I had for Karl Albert Gouda in thirty-two minutes. It was a store, a lamp store on Olympic, not far from the Santa Monica airport.

I was drenched in sweat when I found a parking spot almost half a block away and ran back. The door to the lamp shop was locked and a sign in the window read: "Away for a few minutes. Back soon."

I stood waiting, pulling my shirt from my skin, looking both ways down the street for a madman with a gun or spear. *Soon* was definitely not ten minutes. I have a reasonably good sense of the passage of time, no thanks to my watch. No business had been lost by Karl Albert Gouda in his absence. I was the only potential customer.

I knocked at the door. It rattled. No answer. Something or someone moved deep inside the cavern of a store. I knocked again. Through the window I watched a man in a baggy suit stride from the shadows, past the lamps, and to the door. He was a squat man with bad skin. He had a head of white hair and a look of annoyance on his face.

"What you wan'?" he asked. "We're closed. Can't you read or something?"

"Karl Albert Gouda," I said loudly. "I've got to see him."

"Why?"

"You Gouda?"

"No," the squat man said. "Go away."

"Someone's going to try to kill him in a minute or two."

This got his attention.

"What are you talkin'?"

"He was in *Gone With the Wind*," I tried.

"So?"

"So, someone is killing people who worked on *Gone With the Wind*."

"Get out of here," the squat man said, turning his back and starting to walk away.

"I'm telling the truth," I shouted, rattling the door again.

"Shut up," the squat man said, turning to me again. "You'll call attention. This is a business. What's the matter with you?"

"Let me in," I said.

The squat man held up a hand and said, "Wait. One second. Okay?"

I waited while he disappeared in the depths of the lamp shop. I watched the cars coming past till he returned and opened the door.

"Come on," he said wearily.

He closed the door behind me when I was inside and then hurried back into the depths of the shop without waiting to see if I could keep up with him. He made a strange clanging sound like the Tin Woodsman as he led the way to a door, opened it, and stepped back so I could enter in front of him.

The room was a warehouse, big, with crates and cardboard boxes piled to the ceiling.

"Wait here," the squat man said and left.

I was standing next to an old floor lamp with a green-glass shade. I pulled the chain and the light went on, illuminating the shade. Dark trees, leafless trees with branches like claws, were painted on the underside of the green glass. From a branch of one of the trees a man was dangling, a noose around his neck.

"You like it?" a voice came, waking me from a dream of Universal Studio monsters.

"Fascinating," I said, looking up at a husky man with a satisfied smile on his face.

The man was somewhere in his forties, good teeth, recently barbered straight brown hair. He wore a pair of brown slacks with dark suspenders over a white shirt and brown bow tie.

"Real art," he said. "Gal over in Burbank makes them. She's maybe eighty years old. Can you believe it? All her own inspiration. She did eighteen years hard time some place back east.

Manslaughter. I think it was her brother. Something. Kansas. Ohio. Who knows? One of those places."

"Fascinating," I said.

"You said that already."

"Sorry."

His hands were folded in front of him just below his belly and he was rocking gently on his heels. Behind him the squat man with the white hair and bad complexion stood watching me.

"I don't make a dime on her stuff," the man in suspenders said. "Do I make a dime, Tools?"

"Not one dime, Karl," Tools said flatly.

"Do I care, Tools?"

"Not so's I ever noticed," said Tools.

Karl Gouda took a step toward me and whispered, "I got a passion for art, you see. It's been said my taste runs a little to the morbid. But, I say, who gives a shit? You take it where it goes. You Mormon or something?"

"I'm something, but not a Mormon," I said, looking at the duo facing me.

"If you were, I'd apologize for saying 'shit,' but since you're not, I don't see any need to apologize. You see a need to apologize?"

"No," I said.

"So, what's this shit about someone wanting to kill me?" Gouda said, a look of distaste on his face.

"Charles Larkin, Al Ramone, both extras in *Gone With the Wind*, were murdered in the last three days," I said. "The killer sent a note saying that the next victim would be K.G. and then Lionel Varney. K.G. Your initials."

"And half the county of Los Angeles," Gouda said impatiently.

"But only a few people who worked on *Gone With the Wind*."

I pulled the photograph of Ramone and the soldiers saying hi to Vivien Leigh from my pocket and handed it to him. Gouda looked at the picture.

"Ramone's the one circled in red," I said. "You're all on this nut's list."

"That's me," Gouda said with a sigh, pointing to the photograph.

"And Varney?"

"Don't remember any names," he said. "We were together maybe eight, ten hours. I remember the guy who fell on the sword. This one."

He handed the photograph to me, tapping one of the stubble-covered faces.

"I think we should talk," I said.

"Come with me," Gouda said, reaching over to put a heavy hand on my shoulder.

I moved forward and he guided me toward the back of the store. Tools trailed us, shuffling past rows of lamps. Occasionally, for no reason and with no pattern I could see, Gouda paused to turn a lamp on or off. He talked softly as we walked.

"As you can see, Tiffany is my obsession," he said. "Real Tiffany or really creative stained glass, any period. Delicate, soulful."

He paused to touch the purple-glass shade of a nearby lamp and I staggered to a halt.

"Touch it," he said.

I reached out and touched it.

"Texture," he said intimately. "That's the secret of fine glass, texture."

"*Gone With the Wind*," I reminded him.

"Not if they're properly cared for," he said.

We were moving again, toward the shadows and a partially open door.

"You're an actor," I said.

"I'm what you call an entrepreneur," he countered. "Right, Tools?"

"Hundred percent," came Tools's voice.

We went through the open door. We were in a familiar room, an old room.

"You recognize it?" Gouda asked as Tools closed the door behind us. "Furniture, drapes?"

"I don't . . ."

"Study," he said. "Old O'Hara's study in *Gone With the Wind*. Tara. Not copies. The real stuff. The McCoy. Saturday there's going to be a reunion of some of the cast and crew of the movie. Right on the Selznick lot, in front of the Tara exterior. I understand there are still some pieces left, furniture, paintings. We get first crack at buying it. You working for DeGeorgio or Baumholtz, trying to scare me off of being there to pick up what's left, tell them I'll see them on Saturday. You know what I'm saying here?"

He let go of my shoulder and moved to the wooden chair at the ancient-looking desk and motioned toward an embroidered, rickety-legged armchair. I looked at the door behind me. Tools was leaning against it.

"I'm not gonna ask you why anyone would want to kill me," Gouda said, running an open palm over the surface of the desk. "Truth is, I confess, there are guys who are not well inclined toward me. Women too. A couple or so. Business rivals, DeGeorgio, Baumholtz, and such like. I've got various holdings and interests, right, Tools?"

"A wide variety of interests," Tools agreed.

"Diversification," Gouda said, watching me. "Sit down."

I sat.

"Now," Gouda said. "I'm saying what I'm gonna say because (a) it's true, and (b) I want you impressed. I used to be engaged in contract work for legitimate businesses, corporations, even a union here and there in Detroit, Cleveland, Akron. When they needed people to be reasonable, I used to talk to them, me and Tools and some part-time help. I would talk and they would be reasonable. But I'm more interested in art now, Gothic art. I mention that I have a passion for beauty?"

"Something like that," I said.

"I say it, Tools?"

"Absolutely," Tools agreed.

"And do I have a certain sensitivity for character?"

"Absolutely," Tools agreed. "Very sensitive."

"Could you and me have made it so long through life if I couldn't read through a man or woman who came to me and said the moon is made of shit painted white?"

"Never," said Tools emphatically.

"You," said Gouda, pointing at me, "are telling me shit is white."

"Someone plans to kill you or a woman named Gilmore," I said.

"You said." Gouda sighed. "Who the hell are you?"

"Toby Peters," I said, moving my head to be sure Tools was still leaning against the door.

"You a crackpot?" asked Gouda.

"No," I said.

"You a crackpot?" Tools repeated.

"I'm a private investigator," I said.

"You know anybody named Markowitz, Gamble, Witherspoon," Gouda said, picking up a small porcelain doll.

"Lerner, Romano, Hansen, Arango," Tools went on.

"Any of them send you here with this load of crap?" asked Gouda. "Not that I expect an easy answer."

"Karl," I said with my best smile.

"Mr. Gouda," Tools corrected.

"Mr. Gouda," I amended. "I'm just . . ."

"And some have said I am unjust," he chimed in with a satisfied smile aimed at me and Tools. I couldn't see Tools's reaction. If it wasn't an old favorite of Gouda's, I was sure it went a few miles over Tools.

"Fine," I said, standing up. "I come here maybe to save your life and you play Little Caesar. You're on your own."

Tools was still leaning against the door. I took a step toward him.

"I don't like a guy coming here and telling me someone wants me dead," Gouda said. "It offends me. It makes me think something is going on."

I kept moving toward the door.

"Question, Peters," Gouda said behind me. "How do you think Mr. Nathanson got his nickname?"

I didn't answer.

"Answer," said Gouda and Tools opened his baggy jacket to reveal a holster.

I stopped.

The holster had four pockets. I could see a claw hammer in one pocket and something metal in the other three. Tools was well armed for minor house repairs but I didn't think he could stop me unless he came up with something that fired bullets. He was older than me, a roly-poly barrel.

"Out of the way, Mr. Nathanson," I said.

"Tools sparred with Joe Louis," said Gouda. "When Louis was tuning up for Tony Galento. Tools was a better fighter than Galento. Nothing hurts Tools. That right, Tools?"

"Nothing hurts Tools," Tools agreed, removing an oversized pair of pliers from his holster. "But . . ."

He didn't have to finish.

"No one sent me," I said, turning back to Gouda.

"I'll believe it when Tools has chatted with you a while," he said. "I didn't get to be the most sensitive dealer in Tiffany lamps this side of St. Louis by being incautious."

A buzz. From under Gouda's desk.

"I get it?" asked Tools.

"I get it," said Gouda, rising from the desk and adjusting his tie. "You have a little talk with Mr. Peters and see if maybe he remembers Lerner, DeGeorgio, or Arango."

Gouda moved past me toward the door.

"Where you going?" I asked.

"Customer," he said.

Tools moved away from the door toward me.

"Don't go," I said. "It might be . . ."

Gouda waved his hand at me and went through the door, closing it behind him.

"Tools," I said. "Your boss . . ."

"Karl's not my boss," Tools said, clicking the pliers together like castanets. "We're partners. He's got a passion for lamps with scary stuff, and I got a passion for tools and confession. I was a Catholic when I was a kid."

I backed away toward the desk, looking for a tool of my own.

"What are you now?"

"Bored," he said. "I was happier back east."

There was no way out but through Tools Nathanson. He could see me thinking. Tools shook his head no. I didn't have a choice even if I did have a rotating ball in my stomach that told me the man in front of me was too confident to be bluffing.

I was saved by the gun.

Karl Albert Gouda wasn't.

The shots were close together. Two of them. Tools blinked and turned. He had the door open and was running into the shop before I had taken my first step after him. The fat little son of a gun could move like a welterweight.

By the time I got to the front of the store where Tools was leaning over Karl Gouda near the open front door, I knew I had another victim for the list. I jumped over Gouda and went out the door. A car was going by. Cars were at the curb. A few people were walking across the street. No one was running. I went back inside. Tools was touching Gouda's cheek.

"Karl?" Tools whispered. "You okay? You dead?"

Tools looked up at me. I looked down at Gouda. His chest was covered in blood.

"He's dead," I said. "I warned him. I warned you."

"Like so much shit I'm dead," Gouda said, opening his eyes. His voice was hollow and weak, but he wasn't dead.

Tools was smiling and crying. Gouda tried to sit up.

"Goddamn kid," Gouda said with a cough as Tools, holster clanging, helped him to a sitting position. "Walked in, took two shots. One, two."

And then panic came into his face. He looked around the shop frantically.

"Take it easy, Karl," Tools soothed.

"The lamps," Gouda said. "He get my lamps. I'll rip his heart out."

"I don't think he got any lamps," I said.

"Thank God," said Gouda with a grimace of pain as Tools helped him take off his bloody suspenders, tie, and shirt.

A metal plate gleamed against the fallen man's chest. Tools removed it carefully and Gouda bit his lower lip to keep from screaming.

"Two holes," said Tools. "One made it all the way through. Other looks like it just broke the skin, maybe a rib. What you think, Karl?"

"A rib, definitely a rib," Gouda agreed. Then he looked up at me. "Tools made this. I told you. Some people don't appreciate the work we did in Detroit."

". . . and Kansas City," said Tools. "You want I should get the bullet out, Karl? It's sticking out."

Gouda nodded, looking up at me.

Tools pulled his pliers from his holster and went for the bullet sticking out of Gouda's chest.

"He'll give you blood poisoning," I said.

"My tools are sterile," Tools said, turning on me angrily.

"Sorry," I said.

Tools moved quickly, clamped down on the protruding bullet, looked at Gouda who nodded, and then pulled. Gouda gasped and the bullet flew into the air, crashing into the green-glass lamp with the hanging tree. Gouda closed his eyes and Tools's mouth opened in horror.

I moved to the lamp.

"A little crack," I said.

"I'll find him," said Gouda softly. "I'll find the little shit and . . ."

"What did he look like?" I asked, moving to help Tools get his partner to his feet.

"Like a dead shit," Gouda said. "Why'd you say he was tryin' to kill me?"

"Something to do with *Gone With the Wind*," I said, helping Gouda to a chair near the wall.

Someone came through the door. I turned my head, ready for bullets.

"You have table lamps?" a well-dressed woman said, looking at us curiously.

"I have a bullet in my chest," said Gouda.

The woman looked at me and then at Tools. I don't think she liked what she saw. She turned and left.

"I'll get something to fix you up, Karl," said Tools, touching his partner's shoulder.

"Yeah," said Gouda.

Tools clanked back toward the O'Hara office and I asked again, "What did he look like?"

"A man with no goddamn sensitivity," he said through gritting teeth. "Maybe thirty, not heavy. Losing his hair in front. Dark eyes. Jacket, wearing a jacket with something written on the pocket. I won't forget him."

"Can you take a suggestion?" I asked.

He looked up at me without answering.

"Stay dead for a while. Go on vacation. I'll find the guy. You come back."

"We don't work that way, Peters," he said. "Word gets out Karl Gouda runs and I might as well put a 'shoot me' ad in the *L.A. Times*."

Tools was clanking back like a belled cat. He was carrying a cardboard box. I walked over to the door and closed it. Tools opened the box, pulled out bandages and bottles, removed shears from his belt, and started ministering to his fallen partner.

"I'm going," I said.

"Go," said Gouda, holding up his arms so Tools could wrap the bandage around him. "But we know your name. We can find you."

"We can find you," Tools agreed.

I was about to answer when the plate-glass window shattered a few feet from my head. Lamps and shades exploded as bullets tore through the shop. I hit the floor and cut my chin on broken green glass. Gouda groaned. I lifted my head and saw Tools trying to protect his partner with his own body, but it was too late. There was a hole in Gouda's face.

"He looks more like Swiss than Gouda," came a voice from the sidewalk.

I rolled over, and through the smashed window my eyes met those of the man on the sidewalk. I had seen him about an hour earlier, sitting in Shelly Minck's dental chair. He aimed his pistol at me and was about to pull the trigger when an animal yowled across the street and Tools, clanking and crushing glass underfoot, charged past me.

I got to my feet, cutting my palms on broken glass, as the

young man in the jacket took off down the street and Tools Nathanson took off after him. The man with the gun was at least twenty years younger and wasn't carrying fifteen or twenty pounds of tools.

When I got to the sidewalk, people were starting to move cautiously toward the shop. Not many of them yet. I looked down the street and saw Tools collapsed on his knees about a block away. The killer was nowhere in sight.

I looked back at Gouda. This time he was definitely dead.

Chapter 7

Traffic bustled on Wilshire beyond the open window of Captain Philip Pevsner's office. I sat in the chair opposite Phil's desk and watched him sharpen a pair of pencils, lay out a pad of paper, and rearrange the photographs of his wife, Ruth, my two nephews, Nate and Dave, and my niece, Lucy.

There are some who say my brother and I look alike. And there are others who have better vision or tell the truth. Phil is five years older than I am, a bear with short white hair, hair that had been white since Phil returned from the Great War twenty-five years earlier. We're the same height but his eyes are pale gray and mine are dark brown. He looked like a filled-out version of our father, who had died a few years after Phil came back from France. I looked like the photographs of our mother, who had died when I was born, a fact that Jeremy Butler thought accounted for the lifetime of love-hate, war-peace between us. Phil's tie was open. His eyes were blank and his lips pursed.

"Ruth is doing fine," he said, rolling one of his nice sharp pencils between his palms and looking at me.

I nodded. My sister-in-law, all ninety pounds of her, had come close to dying about a month earlier. The prospect of being alone with three kids all under the age of thirteen must have scared even Phil, and the prospect of being without Ruth, who seemed to understand him, was probably more than he could have handled.

Phil had lived the life of a cop on the verge of a breakdown for two decades. Phil hated criminals, personally. He had been promoted twice, demoted twice; each time, up or down, because he had lost his temper and a suspect had lost teeth or bones. I knew that temper. It was responsible for my flat nose and my looking like a retired and slightly overweight middleweight.

"Kids?" I asked.

"Boys are fine. Lucy's learning to swim."

"Great," I said. "Where's Steve?"

Steve was the thin ghost of a partner my brother haunted the streets of Los Angeles with.

"Vacation," Phil said.

"Where?"

"Seattle, with his sister and mother."

"Great," I said.

"What happened to you?" he asked.

"Happened?"

Phil pointed at my head and hands. There was a Band-aid on my forehead and another on my left palm. The one on my palm wouldn't stick.

"Cut myself on some broken window glass," I said.

Phil nodded, sat back, looked at the sharp point of the pencil in his hand, and took a deep breath.

"We through with crap and Shinola?" he asked.

I shrugged.

"I'm going to say this calmly, Tobias," he said. "I'm going to say this calmly for three reasons. You want to hear my three reasons?"

"Very much," I said, giving him my full attention.

"First, my blood pressure is up. Like dad's. Remember how

he used to get so excited when he argued with Hal Graham? They could argue about whether cranberries were fruits or vegetables. Dad's veins used to pop out on his forehead. His cheeks went red. Sound like someone you know?"

It sounded like Phil Pevsner.

"It killed Dad," said Phil. "It would be a bad joke by the devil if I fell down dead when Ruth was recovering. You know how old Dad was when he died?"

"About . . ." I started, but Phil overlapped me.

"Just the age I am now."

I wasn't sure, but I nodded knowingly.

"Second, I lose perspective when I get excited. I get more interested in smashing than listening. And, I'll admit, sometimes I miss important things."

I was attentive.

"Third, I owe you. When Ruth was in the hospital and you got Bette Davis to see her, Ruth started to get better, to fight her way back. So, you've got my reasons. Now, answer some questions."

"Right," I said.

"Lane Price says you claimed Sheldon Minck hired you to collect an overdue bill from a guy who was murdered in Glendale last night. Lane, as we both know, is a lazy slob, a politician, but he's not deaf. He wants you."

"He was ready to rehire me and make me his right hand yesterday," I said.

"That was before you lied about Minck," said Phil. "Talk. Keep me calm, Tobias. I've got things on my mind. My wife, my family, my job. And I've been wondering where the hell President Roosevelt is. Hasn't been a word in the papers or on the news about him in a week."

"I don't know, Phil," I said.

"But there are some questions you can answer. This is the easiest question I'm going to ask you. The next few are really tough. See if you can answer the question without my asking it."

A horn squawked on Wilshire. Somebody laughed. A car went by playing a song I couldn't quite make out.

"I was protecting my client. He thought Ramone was in danger. A guy named Charles Larkin was killed last week. My client thought the killer might go after Ramone."

"Why?" asked Phil, reasonably.

"They were both extras in *Gone With the Wind*," I explained. "So was Gouda."

"The one in the lamp store," Phil said. "An extra?"

"The one in the lamp store. An extra. And there's another one, Lionel Varney, another extra. I gave you his name when I called and . . ."

"Someone plans to kill every extra in *Gone With the Wind?*" Phil asked.

"Not every extra," I said. "Just the ones who were around the campfire when a fellow thespian got killed."

"That's good. By the time he got done with every extra, the body count would be bigger than Bataan. And this Karen Gilmore you sent me running out to check on. She was in *Gone With the Wind* too?"

"Right," I said.

"But why did you pick her?"

"Initials," I explained. "K.G. The killer said he was going to get K.G. next."

"The killer?"

"Spelling," I said. "The killer is spelling."

And then it hit me. It didn't hit Phil. The killer was Spelling.

"What?" Phil asked.

"What?" I said.

"You just had an idea," said Phil, putting down the pencil.

"No," I said. "Just remembered something I forgot to do. Did you find Varney?"

"There's a Lionel Varney registered at the Carolina Hotel on Sunset. An actor. Been in town for a few days. How would you describe my attitude, Tobias? Right now. Calm?"

"Remarkably calm," I agreed.

There was a knock at the door behind me. The door opened.

"Captain," came a voice.

Something sailed past my head and crashed into the door as it closed.

"I told you to leave me alone till I came out," Phil shouted. Then he turned to me.

"Phil," I said calmly.

"I'm fine," he said, pointing a pencil at me. "Stopped drinking coffee. I'm eating cucumber-and-tomato sandwiches for lunch. Who's your client?"

"Phil, how many times do we have to go over this? I can't tell you my client's name without his or her permission."

"Where does it say that in any law book, any city, county, or state statute?" Phil said, placing his hands flat on his desk.

"I think your blood pressure is going up, Phil," I said softly, wondering if I should make a break for the door.

"Where does it say it, Toby?" he said evenly.

"Law of the Jungle. Code of the West. A Man's Gotta Do. Come on, Phil. What have I got to sell but a hard head and a closed mouth? My client didn't kill anybody. You know I didn't kill anybody."

"The chief of police of Glendale wants you on a possible homicide or withholding evidence," said Phil, standing up and turning his back on me.

Phil's hands were knotted behind his back.

"Between you and me, strictly off the record?" I asked.

"I can't do that," Phil said, with a distinct pause between each word.

"You can, Phil. You just don't want to."

He turned suddenly like a wild bear, face red, teeth clenched. I jumped out of my chair and moved back toward the door. Phil closed his eyes, took a deep breath. His face returned to its normal color.

"Off the record," Phil said.

"Clark Gable."

I was standing behind the chair now.

"Clark Gable?"

"Yes."

"Gable's in England," said Phil, loosening his tie even more and glaring at me.

"No, he's back for a few days. No one knows. He's at his house in Encino. Jeremy Butler's with him. I've got the number. I think someone may want to kill him. Spelling, the guy who shot Gouda."

"Why?" Phil asked. "Why does this guy Spelling want to kill Clark Gable?"

"I don't know," I said. "Give me a few days and maybe I'll find out."

"And maybe more people will be murdered."

"Can you protect everyone who worked on *Gone With the Wind*?"

"Friday," said Phil, sitting at his desk. "You got till Friday."

"Thanks, Phil," I said.

His eyes were closed now.

"Phil?"

"I'm meditating," he said.

"Medi—?"

"Just close the goddamn door and get the hell out of here. Friday you come with answers or I find you, manacle you, and personally drag you to Glendale."

I didn't say thanks. I didn't say anything. I opened the door and left. I took a cab back to Gouda's lamp store. A crew of men and women in overalls were sweeping up glass and boarding up windows.

Tools Nathanson was standing in front on the sidewalk, a blank look on his face, a hammer in his hand, watching the crew sweep away his partner's passion.

I got in my Crosley and headed for the Farraday Building.

Chapter 8

The Carolina Hotel was top dollar. A girl in a cute red-and-gold short-skirted uniform, one of those little bellboy caps tied around her chin, took the keys to my Crosley and gave me a grin. I gave her a buck for not noticing I wasn't driving a Lincoln.

An old man in a red-and-gold uniform, long pants, opened the hotel door for me and I walked into one of the great lobbies of America. Mosaic-tile floors with flower pattern, gold walls, and plump furniture in little nooks made private by tall ferns and plants. Parrots gurgled in a dozen cages. People bustled in and out, talking business, making deals, trying not to notice if they were being noticed.

I walked the half mile across the lobby and informed the tuxedoed clerk that Mr. Varney was expecting me. The clerk, who looked as if he never needed a shave, did something with his head that might have been a nod, or maybe he just closed his eyes for an instant in acknowledgment.

I was wearing a zippered tan Windbreaker, dark slacks, a white shirt fraying only slightly at the collar, and a tie that came close to matching the dark of my trousers. In New York, I'd definitely be sent to the service entrance. In Los Angeles, hundred thousand-dollar-a-year executives dressed the way I was dressed, even for business meetings. Working-man casual was in. Only actors dressed in suits.

The clerk stepped discreetly back out of my hearing and picked up a house phone. He was replaced by a near-duplicate ready to greet the next inquiry. Nobody inquired. Clerk Two didn't smile. Clerk One returned and said, "Room 304. Mr. Varney is expecting you."

Which was what I had said.

I said thanks and turned in search of the elevator. I found it in a niche beyond where three men and a woman were sitting forward and whispering at the top of their voices.

The Carolina had an elevator operator with a smile of perfect teeth, who wore an appropriate gold-and-red uniform and looked a little like Jane Powell. She took me up to the third floor and opened the door for me.

The Carolina was Hollywood class.

The red-and-gold carpeting was thick and clean-smelling. The walls were lined with paintings and watercolors of California mountains, beaches, and forests. No movie stars. No reproductions of famous paintings by long-dead Dutchmen.

The door to 304 was open.

"Peters, come in," Varney called, and I came in and closed the door behind me.

The room was big. More carpets. A sofa. A pair of matching stuffed chairs with a glass-top coffee table between them. An open bar against one wall and balcony looking out on the swimming pool and Beverly Hills.

Varney was at the bar, fresh white shirt open at the collar, sleeves rolled up, slacks creased, and shoes shined. A well-trimmed wave of graying hair sat on a pleasantly Indian-looking tan face. He didn't look anything like the dusty bitter Confederate soldier I'd met five years earlier.

"Drink?" he asked, holding up a glass of dark liquid over ice to show me he was having one.

"Pepsi, if you've got it," I said, moving to the window to get a better look at two tan girls taking lessons from a man in white.

"Meet it. Don't beat it," the tennis pro said in a booming voice three floors below.

I could hear the girls giggle. I could hear ice tinkle behind me.

"Pepsi, on the rocks," Varney said, handing me the glass.

"Thanks."

He looked down at the pro and the girls and sighed.

"Things change," he said.

"Some things," I said.

I turned and Varney pointed to one of the chairs with his free hand. I sat.

"Last time you saw me I was feeling more than a bit sorry for myself and wondering if I should spend my last few dollars and head back to selling women's shoes in Moline."

He sat and looked around.

"And now," he continued. "There's a bedroom through there and a bathroom as big as a small destroyer beyond it."

"What's your story?" I asked.

"Went to New York," he said, after a long sip of golden liquid. "Did well on the radio. Tried the theater. Lucky. I came when the leading men were shipping out and the choice just off Broadway was babies or old farts for leading men. Two years earlier and I would have hit the skids and headed for Moline. Never to be heard from or cared about. I was an only kid. Mother and father dead. Relatives are all in Finland. Never married. Studio's going to have to be creative in making a biography that will get a line or two with Hedda."

"I gather you've got a movie contract," I said.

"Three pictures. Universal. All Bs, but I'm the star. God, I was lucky. Associate producer named Cantor caught me in something called *Is This Seat Taken?* I had a death scene and I was feeling perfect that night. I . . ."

He was looking at me when he stopped and he must have seen something that told him I hadn't come to admire his triumphant return.

"What is it?" he said, putting down his drink.

"The night I met you. Burning of Atlanta. Man got killed."

"I remember," he said. "Crazy accident."

"One for Ripley," I agreed. "You scare easy?"

"Normal," he said, cautiously watching my eyes.

"Looks like someone's killing off all of you," I said.

"All of? . . ."

"The extras playing Confederate soldiers. The ones who were there when that guy got killed."

I fished out the photograph and handed it to him. He held it in both hands for a few seconds before saying, "That's me. And this one, right here," he said, turning the photograph to me. "He's the one who died. Lord God, I had all but forgotten that night. Do the police know? What are they doing?"

I took the photograph back and said, "The police know. They're doing what they can do. Remember his name? The man who got killed?"

"No. Wait. Maybe it was Lang, or Long. I don't . . . someone is killing us? Why?"

I had finished my Pepsi but I didn't feel like asking for another.

"You heard something. Saw something. Said something. Did something. Best guess is that the guy who got killed was murdered and the killer's spent five years worrying that he might have been seen, or said something to give him away."

"Five years?" Varney said.

"Doesn't make a hell of a lot of sense," I agreed. "But when you're crazy, you don't have to make sense. One of the good things about being crazy."

Varney got up now and was pacing the room. I listened to the ice click in his glass and watched him think.

"I've only been back in town for two weeks," he said. "The studio hasn't done any publicity. How could this person know I was even here?"

"Crazy doesn't mean stupid," I said.

Lionel Varney snorted, shook his head, and looked at his melting ice.

"The goddamn irony," he said. "I work a lifetime for a break and some lunatic wants to kill me. Wants to kill me and I don't even know why."

"You want advice?" I asked.

Varney stopped pacing and looked down at me in the chair.

"Get a room under another name. Don't tell anyone where you are but me. I'll stay in touch and tell you when it's safe."

He was shaking his head even before I had finished.

"Can't," he said. "I'm riding some good reviews and reports and spending goodwill fast. I can't tell Universal I have to hide for who knows how long. And Saturday. Saturday I've been invited to sit at Universal's table for the Academy Awards dinner with Walter Wanger, Jon Hall, Turhan Bey, and Maria Montez. Then there's a publicity reunion at Selznick, in front of Tara. Reporters, cameras, big names. Universal's planning the official announcement of my contract and my first starring role. I'm not risking that, Peters. I'd rather get some protection and take my chances."

"Suit yourself," I said, standing up and handing him my glass. He had one in each hand now.

"I can't believe this," he said.

"Believe it, Lionel," I said. "Keep your door locked and pay someone big with a gun to stand outside it. And try to be calm."

I moved to the door.

"Be calm," he said with a sarcastic laugh. "That's easy for you to say. You're not on this madman's list."

"I think I am, Lionel. I think I am. I'll call you when I have something, or more questions."

Varney didn't show me out. I made my own way down the stairs. I couldn't face Jane Powell's big white teeth and smile. I wove my way through the lush jungle of the Carolina Hotel lobby, heard a parrot squawk behind me, and got onto the driveway.

"Car?" asked a young man in the familiar uniform.

"Crosley," I said. "Sort of brown."

"We only have one Crosley on the lot," he said politely and hurried off.

I could hear tennis balls hitting and echoing as I waited. I could hear the hum of traffic on Sunset. I could hear my heart beating. I had a sudden urge to visit my niece and nephews or find Dash and see if he'd sit on my lap a while. I had a strong wish to go home, but I had a long day in front of me and Clark Gable's money to spend.

I parked behind the Farraday and gave Big Elmo two bits to watch the Crosley. Big Elmo was the latest in a string of derelicts who lived in the alley behind the building. There have been poets, fools, crazies, grumblers, dreamers, the dazed. One guy had returned for two seasons. Most hung around a few months, sleeping in rusted-out abandoned cars. All were willing to take a quarter or two to watch the Crosley and keep it safe from each other.

Big Elmo wasn't big. He was a straw in an oversized yellow dress shirt cut short at the sleeves. The shirt was dirty. Elmo was dirty. His wisps of hair were unruly, but his manners were the best.

"Think I need a shave?" he asked, pocketing my coins.

"Wouldn't hurt," I said.

Elmo looked around his alley domain. Cars beeped and chugged on Main Street beyond the Farraday. Elmo seemed to listen and then touch his face.

"Just need another tomorrow," he said. "And who'm I trying to impress, I ask you."

"You've got a point," I said. "But if you put the shave together with a bath, some clean clothes from Hy's or Chi Chi's Slightly Worn on Hoover, you might be able to line up a job."

"Had one once," Elmo said with a smile. "Makes me itch. Got no patience. Most guys out here . . ." He looked around, but there weren't any guys. "Most guys have a story. What they were. What they walked away from. You know?"

"I know," I said.

Elmo jangled the coins in his pocket.

"I got no story. No ambition. What the hell. You're born one day. Sixty, seventy years later you're dead. You know?"

"I know," I said.

Elmo shook his head.

"So," he went on, "the way I figure it, why waste the sixty, seventy with work, trying to get something you can't keep anyway. I'm not starvin'. I'm not cold or wet most days. I get plenty of time to read over at the library or wherever."

"I get your point, Elmo."

"You think I could really get a job?" he asked, looking away from me. "I mean if I cleaned up okay?"

"Lot of jobs, Elmo. The gravy's in the navy."

"Cash money and room with a door," he said, more to himself than me. "Might be I'd want to try it. Never tried it."

"You know Manny's around the corner on Main," I said. "He's looking for a dishwasher. There's a sign in his window. I'll put in a word for you."

"Maybe," said Elmo.

I went to the Crosley, opened the door with my key, and reached into the cramped back seat. My gym bag was there. I pulled it out while Elmo watched me find a rolled-up pullover shirt and safety razor already loaded with a fresh Chancellor single-edged blade. I handed shirt and razor to Elmo, who took them with dignity.

"You don't like it, you can always quit," I said.

"What about your car?"

"I'll take a chance," I said.

I left Elmo standing in the rubble behind the Farraday, deciding if he had the heart to take a step into the 1940s. I wanted to feel good. I wanted to feel as if I was saving a lost soul, but I wasn't sure. I also wanted to take the edge off of what I was feeling, a combination of excitement, fear, and anger. They were still with me when I went through the back entrance to the Farraday and closed the door behind me.

When you step into the Farraday from the back door, you're plunged into a darkness without shadows. I've tripped over sleeping bums and debris. I've stepped into slick splots of who-knows what. Jeremy and Alice worked with buckets, brawn, and chemicals to stay ahead of the jungle, but it was a never-ending job, and time off for the baby or poetry only meant the streets would slouch under the door or through a window for a new assault.

I moved around a corner and made my way to the lobby door, marked with a red bulb. I pushed into the lobby and felt the same tug I always feel. Something a little sad, something I knew someday I would miss. The open tile space with a wide stairway and dark-metal railings climbing floor by floor to the sixth floor and the dirty skylight. The iron elevator next to the stairway, clanging gently from a sourceless breeze. Voices one-two-five-six flights up through the doors marked as the homes of one-man and one-woman businesses that couldn't make it in the nicer buildings a few blocks north.

Something moved above me as I headed for the stairway. I looked up and saw Alice Pallis at the first-floor railing, holding Natasha in her arms. The baby was patting her mother's head with a pudgy palm.

"Jeremy told me to look for you," Alice said. "He wants you to call him in Encino."

"Thanks, Alice," I said.

"Toby, I asked you and you said you'd leave Jeremy out of your work."

"I'm sorry," I said, starting up the stairs. "I don't think there's any . . ."

". . . and we figured out your puzzle," she said.

I kept coming up the stairs. I didn't have the heart to tell her that I'd figured it out too, at least most of it.

"Great," I said as she moved toward the stairway landing.

"If it's not French," a man's voice shouted from above us, "I can't sell it. You get me French, I'll get you cash."

I got to the first floor, not even panting. Natasha reached for me and Alice handed her over. She smelled like innocence and baby powder.

"The initials of each victim," Alice said. "Charles Larkin, Al Ramone, Karl Gouda, C.L.A.R.K. G. And in his last note, he says he 'began lame but I'll end able.' ABLE. Clark Gable."

Natasha was pulling at my ear. She wasn't more than four months old, but she had inherited her father and mother's strength. Alice reached over, removed her hand from my ear, kissed Natasha's palm, and took her back. She immediately began to pat her mother's head again and gurgle.

"Your killer is issuing a warning to Clark Gable, taunting him," Alice said. "Maybe wanting him to feel responsible for the deaths of these men for no other reason than to spell the name of a movie star."

"I don't like crazies," I said.

"Who does unless they're funny?" she said.

A grinding machine sound began a floor or two above us. We had to raise our voices.

" 'I'll be there e'er the Ides and right those wrongs and claim his prize,' " Alice went on. "Jeremy thinks he wrote that to let you know that he plans to do something before the fifteenth, the ides. Jeremy had me read *Julius Caesar*. Caesar is warned about the ides, but he ignores the warning, and then he's murdered on the ides, stabbed by former friends."

"The king," I said. "Gable's called the king."

"So, it could be that he plans to murder Clark Gable before the fifteenth," said Alice. " 'My father wept to be so cut from fortune, fame deservéd.' Suggestion, Toby. We think his father didn't get something that could have made him rich and famous, something about Clark Gable. And he plans to get his revenge before the fifteenth. Jeremy thinks your killer's father had something to do with *Gone With the Wind*. All three victims had something to do with the film."

All this I knew, but I didn't have the heart to tell Alice. Natasha was solemnly exploring her mother's nostrils. Alice paid no attention.

"We're still puzzled by some of his comments," Alice said. "Who am I? Just ask what I am d.o.i.n.g."

"Spelling," I said. "He's Spelling. His name is Spelling."

"How can anyone be expected to figure that out?" Alice said, nestling her nose into Natasha's stomach. The baby giggled.

"Maybe we're not supposed to figure it out till it's too late," I said.

"Then why play the game?" Alice asked.

"To show he's smarter than me, smarter than Gable," I said. "To make us feel that we should have figured it out, when it's too late."

Alice gently put Natasha's head against her neck and patted her back softly to calm the giggling baby.

"He's sick, Toby," Alice said. "I've got to go change Natasha and give her a nap."

"He's sick, Alice," I agreed.

Alice started to walk away and then turned to me, her homely face serious.

"I don't want Jeremy near him," she said.

"I'll . . ."

"Listen," she said, shifting the baby slightly so she could hold her with one hand while she plucked a sheet of paper from the pocket of her dress. Natasha stirred and did a baby sigh and went quiet again. Alice shook open the sheet and read,

> "Blake thought he found God
> in the wake of a tiger, the burst of sun, the flower,
> Shakespeare in the wit of words
> the recognition of the power
> of well-put passion.
> Pound pounds his Nazi chains
> against the steel drum of fear
> while I take issue, take pains
> to find the postured dignity
> that holds my hand through doubt
> and lets me reach back with earthy
> strength to those I love and say,
> 'Take my hand for I will hold you fast
> through time to come and which has past.
> We are not first but we'll not be last.'"

"Well?" Alice challenged, folding the sheet with one hand and dropping it back in her pocket.

"Impressive," I said.

"If Jeremy gets hurt, Toby, I'll crush your head with my bare hands. I will."

"I know, Alice."

There was nothing more to say. She and the still-giggling

baby vanished into the shadows, and I went back to the stairway and made my way up to the office of Sheldon Minck and Toby Peters.

There were voices beyond the waiting room: Shelly's, though it seemed unnatural somehow. The other voice was a woman's. I opened the door and found Shelly standing next to a girl who stood a good six inches taller than him. She was slender, dark, with a short Louise Brooks haircut and wearing a green dress with fluffy sleeves. She also wore a smile and too much makeup.

Shelly was showing her drawings and trying to keep his glasses from slipping off as he pointed to details with the dead end of his cigar.

". . . in your office," he said, pointing back at my office.

She saw me first. Then Shelly's eyes came up, filled with magnified guilt behind the thick lenses. The girl smiled. She was cute, maybe a little empty, but cute.

"Oh, Toby," Shelly said, quickly dropping his drawings on the dental chair. "This is Mrs. Gonsenelli, Violet."

Violet Gonsenelli held out her hand. I stepped forward to take it. It was slender, warm, and definitely did not belong, along with that face and body, in the less-than-spotless offices of Minck and Peters.

"Pleasure," she said.

"Mrs. Gonsenelli applied for the receptionist job," Shelly explained. "I told her the ad was old, but she has some great ideas and she needs the job."

"Husband's in Europe," she explained. "Fighting the Nazis."

"Best reason to be there," I said.

"Business is growing, Toby," Shelly said nervously. "Wouldn't be bad to have someone keep track of things, straighten up."

"You were talking about my office," I said.

"Your . . ." Shelly began, looking at my office door as if he had never seen it before. "Well, it was just a possibility, you know. Violet would need an office and . . ."

Violet looked confused.

"Mildred," I said. "Mildred gets one look at Violet and she's on the way to Reno."

"This is business," Shelly said with indignation. "Mildred would just have to understand."

"Mildred?" Violet asked.

"Mrs. Minck," I explained.

Violet nodded in understanding. I had the feeling this was not the first job interview foiled by a Mildred Minck.

"Maybe I'd better go," Violet said.

"Wait," said Shelly. "Toby?"

"Your marriage, Dr. Minck," I said. "We can clear out the waiting room for Violet, put in a small desk. Patients and clients can wait in the hall. You put two or three chairs out there and maybe, who knows, if you're lucky, they won't get stolen. You'd better check with Jeremy and Alice to see if they'll let you do it."

Shelly was beaming.

"I don't . . ." Violet began.

"You don't have to," Shelly said. "You just make appointments, answer the phone, straighten up, learn about the dental business. I tell you what. I'll train you to be a dental assistant. Clean teeth, X rays. A career."

"What about Mrs. Minck?" Violet said, looking at me.

I shrugged.

"I got it," said Shelly, snapping his pudgy fingers. "Toby hires you. You're his idea. I pay my share of your salary, but . . ."

"You pay all of Mrs. Gonsenelli's salary and she works for both of us," I said.

"But . . ."

"And I give you permission to tell Mildred I hired her," I threw in.

"It's a deal," said Shelly.

"I don't know," said Violet.

Violet was cute. Violet could be more than cute. This was probably a rotten idea.

"Forty a month, plus a free white smock," said Shelly. "Good pay, career opportunity. Flexible working hours."

Violet looked at me.

"Can we make it a kind of trial?" she said, looking back at Shelly again. "Till I can ask Angelo."

"Angelo?"

"My husband. I'll write to him tonight."

"Angelo Gonsenelli?" Shelly said to himself.

"Middleweight contender," I said. "Went six rounds with Tony Zale in '42. Zale couldn't put him down."

"Angelo has heart," Violet said, nodding her head.

"And a wonderful nickname," I added. "Mad Angelo Gonsenelli."

"When do I start?" she asked brightly, her bright-red lips parted to show amazingly white and even teeth that would be the envy of any potential patient.

"Start?" said Shelly in a daze.

"Tomorrow will be fine," I said. "Dr. Minck will help you get things in shape."

"Nine?" she asked.

"Perfect," I said.

And Violet Gonsenelli, wife of Mad Angelo Gonsenelli, was out the door, heels clicking as she headed for the elevator.

"You knew," Sheldon said, moving to his dental chair and sitting on top of his drawings.

"When I heard her name," I said brightly.

"Cruel, Toby," he said.

"Sheldon, you were about to give her my office. Where the hell did you think I was going to go?"

Shelly adjusted his glasses, looked at his cigar, and shrugged.

"I like your idea about turning the waiting room into a reception area–office."

"Thanks," I said. "Give Mildred my best tonight."

"She hates you, Toby," Shelly said.

"Lucky for you, Shel," I said. "I'm mad about her. I'd steal her out from under you and run with her in my arms all the way to Tijuana if she'd have me." Mildred was odds-on favorite to win the witch-in-the-middle contest, if the May Company sponsored a Halloween event.

"You're being sarcastic," Shelly said, lighting his cigar.

I took a step toward Shelly and said, "I want to know about Spelling."

Shelly blinked at me. "What's to know? A few rules but mostly memorizing," he said. "You got a problem, keep a dictionary on your desk. Sometimes, Toby, you come up with the damndest . . . what happened to your head?"

He pointed to the small Band-aid on my forehead. I pulled it off and threw it toward the overflowing white trash can near the sink.

"This morning," I said, "someone you know tried to kill me."

"Mildred?"

"Your patient. A guy named Spelling."

"Good teeth," said Shelly.

"And good aim," I went on. "He shot a man this morning. Stabbed one last night and killed another one three days ago. I think he's also planning to kill me and Clark Gable."

"Just because I made a little mistake with a novocaine injection?" asked Shelly.

"No, Shel, because he's out of his mind. I think he came here this morning to find me, to follow me. I think he's playing a game."

"No wonder his teeth were in such good shape," said Shelly with a stroke of understanding that made no sense to me.

"Shel, I doubt if it will do any good, but I'd like to see your card on Mr. Spelling."

"That's confidential information, Toby," Shelly said seriously. "Patient-doctor, priest-confessional, lawyer-client, that sort of thing."

"Give me the card, Shel, or I'll call Mildred and tell her about your hiring a receptionist who looks better than Rita Hayworth."

Shelly leapt from his chair in indignation and stumbled forward, almost falling to the floor.

"Blackmail," he sputtered.

"The card, Sheldon," I said.

Shelly gathered his dignity, adjusted his soiled smock, and moved to the file cabinet next to the cluttered, dripping sink. He opened it, looked at me in the hope that I would change my mind, and then came up with a card.

"Right here on top," he said. "Chronological system. Latest patient on top."

He pushed the drawer shut and came to me with the card held out.

"Thanks, Shel," I said, looking at the card.

The name he had given was Victor Spelling. There was something vaguely familiar about the address. There was something very familiar about the place of birth. I turned the card to Shelly.

"Read it, Shel."

"Tara, Twelve Oaks, Georgia," he read. Then he looked up. "So?"

I went on reading. According to the card, Spelling was thirty-one, was five-eleven, weighed 190, and had no cavities.

I brushed past Shelly, went to my office.

Behind me Shelly was mumbling, "What did I do?"

I kicked my door closed and picked up the phone. Sarason at vehicle registration wasn't in, but Grace Smull was.

"Price is up, Peters," she said. "Five bucks. And I haven't got much time."

"Victor Spelling," I said.

I gave her the address. I could hear voices in the vehicle-registration office, but I couldn't make out the words. Grace Smull was back on in about two minutes.

"You have my home address?" she asked.

"In my notebook," I said.

"Read it back to me," she said.

I dug my notebook out of my pocket, flipped through the pages, and found her name right under Ida Sarason.

"Five bucks," she said. "Cash. In the mail today or drop it off."

"I understand," I said.

"First, your Victor Spelling's address is the Carlton Arms Hotel," she said. "Second, he has a nineteen thirty-eight Ford business coupe registered to him, license plate four-zero-three-eight."

"I hate to ask, Grace, but could you check on registrations for any other Spellings?"

"Five bucks more," she said.

"Five bucks more," I agreed.

"There are four Spellings with motor vehicles registered in Los Angeles County," she said.

"That was fast."

"I anticipated," she said. "You want to hear? You want to complain? Cost you no more to listen. Cost you another five to complain."

"I'm listening."

She gave me the names of the four Spellings on her list and their addresses. She even gave me the year and model of their cars.

"Thanks, Grace," I said. "Tell Sarason I said hello."

"Tell her yourself," said Grace. "I tell her and she expects a finder's fee."

"You're all heart, Grace," I said.

"It's a hard world out there, Peters. And I'm alone with a sick mother and a teenager to feed. I save my heart for them. Ten dollars. Cash. In the mail."

She hung up and I took out my wallet, found two fives, dug around for an envelope, and had the payment ready to go in about two minutes. I made a note of the expense in my book and got up to leave. Then I remembered Jeremy's call.

I found Gable's number and called. It rang eight times before Jeremy answered.

"It's Toby," I said. "What's up?"

"He called here," Jeremy said. "Your madman."

"His name, maybe even his real name, is Spelling," I said. "What did he want?"

"He insisted on talking to Gable. Told him that he had killed K.G. and said the puzzle was complete. I'm afraid you were right to be concerned, Toby. It is my conclusion that he plans to murder Mr. Gable."

Then I heard a familiar voice saying, "Let me have that thing." Then Gable was on the phone. "Peters. I want that maniac found and I want to be there when he is. I want to wring his neck with my bare hands."

"I've got some . . ." I tried, but he was going strong.

"He said things about my . . . things. The crazy son of a bitch thinks I was responsible for doing something to his father. I have no idea who his father is or was. I want him, Peters. Now, what, if anything, do you know?"

I told him. About Gouda, Alice and Jeremy's solution to the killer's puzzle, the killer's name—real or not—and his giving the Carlton Arms as his home address for his vehicle registration. I also told him about my meeting with Phil.

"I don't like sitting around here," Gable said. "And I don't want him killing any more people and holding me responsible. You're telling me that the crazy son of a bitch is killing people simply because their initials spell my name?"

"Looks that way," I said.

"Find him, Peters."

"I'm working on it," I said.

"Work fast, Peters. For God's sake, work fast."

He hung up and so did I. I wasn't through making calls. I tried Wally Hospodar's number in Calabasas. After five or six rings, a woman answered.

"My name's Peters," I said. "Can I speak to Wally?"

"He doesn' live here anymore," the woman said in a decidedly Spanish accent.

"I'm a friend," I said. "I have to reach him. If . . ."

"Tell you the same thing I told the other one," she said wearily. "He lives someplace downtown L.A. in a bottle of Scotch. Spends his life and his pension in bars."

"Any bars in particular?"

"Melody Lounge or Gardens. Something like that," she said.

"I know the place. You said someone else called looking for Wally?"

"Yesterday. Day before," she said.

"Thanks," I said.

"You see Wally you tell him something for me?"

"Sure."

"Tell him Angelina loves him and he should not come home."

"I'll tell him," I promised and the phone went dead.

When I got back into Shelly's office, he was putting his drawings in a neat stack as he searched for some uncluttered place to put them.

"Spelling owes me money for the cleaning," Shelly said. "You think he'll pay his bill?"

"I wouldn't count on it, Shel," I said.

"Dentistry is a risky business," he said, depositing the drawings back on the dental seat.

"Riskier with Violet Gonsenelli sitting in the reception room," I said. "I've gotta go, Shel. I'm going to pick up a couple of tacos at Manny's and I don't think I'll be back today. I'll call you for messages."

"At least when Violet's here, I won't have to take messages," he grumbled.

"Good-bye, Shel," I said, opening the door.

"Wait," Shelly called, peeling off his smock. "I'll take a lunch break."

I noticed two things when we got to Manny's. First, the Dishwasher Wanted sign was gone. Second, the place was crowded. Manny's wasn't that big to start with. Four booths and a counter with a dozen red leatherette swivel stools. Two cops were just getting up from the counter. Shelly and I slid in past them and took their places.

A hand came out and started removing the dirty dishes. I looked up. It was Elmo, strands of hair in place, face shaved, my pullover shirt under his white apron.

"That was fast," I said.

"No time to change my mind," Elmo said, working away. "Job's easy. Keep it clear. Clean it up. You want your two bits back? I can't watch your car and work a job."

"Forget it," I said.

Elmo hurried away with the dishes, and Manny, a lump of a man with a weary look on his face, leaned over to us, his newspaper open to the crossword puzzle.

"I read the papers every day," he said with the rasp of a child of the teens doomed to the results of a bad tonsillectomy. "But . . . thirty-two across, 'Inhabitants of Europe's un-

derbelly,' twenty-seven across, 'New leader of the House of
Commons.' Wait. This one I can get, 'Preacher McPherson.'
Aimee Semple. Second wife and me, her name was Ernestina,
used to go to the Four Square Gospel Church over on Glendale Boulevard near Sunset, Echo Park. Thousand, maybe two
thousand packed in. I remember Sister Aimee saying, 'Where
there's sin there's salvation. Ernestina took her to heart. Never
got through to me though. Got no imagination. Third and
present wife's got no imagination either. Works out better
that way."

"How's Elmo working out?" I asked.

"Too soon to tell," said Manny. "Says he's your friend."

"Says right," I said.

"Too soon to tell," Manny said again. "What happened to
your head?"

"Patient of Shelly's tried to kill me."

"Java, Manny," a woman called from the end of the counter.

"Comin' up," Manny called back and then to us, seriously,
"R.A.F.'s pounding the Nazis in France, Netherlands. You see
the *Times*?"

"Not today," I said.

"I'll have the three-taco special and coffee," said Shelly.

"British stopped Rommel in North Africa," Manny went
on, ignoring Shelly. "And Montgomery is counterattacking.
Looks good in Africa, Europe, and the Russians aren't doing
so good today."

"Java, Manny," called the woman.

"Customers," Manny said and eased away. He hadn't taken
my order. Didn't need to. Unless I told him otherwise, he
brought me a Pepsi and a pair of tacos.

The guy on the stool next to me hit me with an elbow,
apologized, and went back to his business.

Then the raspy voice came behind me over the chatter and
the radio which Manny had turned on to the news.

"Hand."

"Juanita, I don't . . ."

Juanita reached over Shelly and took my hand, spinning me around on the stool.

You couldn't miss Juanita. Orange-and-gold billowing dress, colored beads around her neck, jangling bracelets and silver earrings the size of a burrito. Juanita's hair was dark and wild, her weight was her own business, and her age was somewhere over the rainbow. Juanita had an office in the Farraday. Juanita was a seer. Don't make the mistake of calling her a fortune teller. Many had slipped. All had regretted it.

"Nothing new here," she said, running a red fingernail across my palm. "But you're givin' off something. Like my second husband Ivan just before he went north, never to be heard from again."

The news blared, customers babbled, dishes clanked, and Juanita said, "You got his game wrong, Toby."

"Who?"

"Who?" she repeated sarcastically. "Whoever's giving you a hard time. Whoever's playin' a game with you. He's got his finger up your you-know-what and he's spinnin' you around, pointing your head the wrong places."

"Thanks," I said.

"The stars," she said, looking into my eyes. "All the stars will be in one place as you stand in the grove. Someone wants you to go to the grove. He wants you watching stars in the grove."

"The grove?" Shelly asked as Manny plopped the tacos and drinks on the counter.

"The grove," she repeated.

"Orange grove?" I tried.

"A grove where the fruit is hard as a turtle shell," she said. "Don't go to this grove, Toby. Juanita is tellin' you straight from the heart. Don't go. Finish your tacos and I'll read the crumbs. Maybe there's more."

"Another time, Juanita," I said.

"Suit yourself," she said with a jangling shrug.

"How's your sister?"

"Okay," she said. "Arthritis. Bad season. Watch yourself, Toby."

"I will, Juanita," I said.

She bustled out of Manny's, humming something I didn't recognize. Juanita had a way of being right about things, but I'd never been able to make sense of anything she told me till it was too late. It's like being told the winner of the Kentucky Derby in a code you know you can't break.

"You believe in that stuff?" Shelly asked.

I swiveled back around and reached for my first taco.

"Wipe your face, Shel. You got sour cream on your chins."

Chapter 9

Victor Spelling was, according to the desk clerk, a resident of the Carlton Arms. It took another five bucks of Clark Gable's money for me to find out that his room number was 342, that he had been at the Carlton Arms since January second. Spelling paid on time, said little, and often walked out in a tux and tie.

"Think he's a waiter at some big restaurant," the clerk said, trying to earn his bribe or urge me into an even bigger one. "Don't know which one, Toby."

It was late in the morning on Monday and business was slow. Only one person, an old man in a shaggy brown suit, was sitting in the lobby. The old man was sitting in a red-leather chair, his chin forward against his chest, his eyes closed.

The furniture was all red leather in the Carlton Arms lobby. A trio of ceiling fans ground around, redistributing the muggy air. The clerk dabbed daintily at his brow with a handkerchief.

The clerk was named Sandy Mixon. He had a round, red face, a thick neck, very little hair, oversized teeth, and a great desire to please. We had never, as far as either of us knew, met before this morning, yet I was his old pal Toby, and he was . . .

"Sandy, what if I told you Vic and I were old friends, high school . . ."

"He's about ten years younger than you, Toby."

"I was slow in high school, Sandy. Math is my nemesis."

The old man asleep in the red-leather chair snorted. Both Mixon and I looked at him. The old man's eyes opened wide. He looked around, confused, saw us, blinked, and went back to sleep.

"Can you add five more to what you've already put in the pot?"

"What'll it buy me?" I asked.

"A bellboy who'll open room 342, a Band-aid for that little cut on your forehead, and my further assurance that you are not deficient in your math skills," said Mixon. "I taught arithmetic to third-graders in Fresno. That was three months in '37. Worst winter of my life, and you're talking to a man who grew up and grew cold in Hibbing, Minnesota."

"Keep the Band-aid," I said, peeling off another five and handing it to him. "It gives me character."

Mixon examined the bill, flattened it with the side of his hand, folded it, and wedged it into his jacket pocket with the other bills.

"For free," Mixon said, leaning forward and dabbing his neck with his handkerchief. "Another guy was looking for Spelling today. Short, big arms, white hair, bad skin, worse attitude."

"Tools Nathanson," I said.

"Name rings no bells," said Mixon, standing erect. "Slow man with a dollar. Said he'd be back. Said I should say nothing to Spelling about his having been around. He slipped me three Washingtons. I said I'd shut up. Truth to tell, I don't talk to Mr. Spelling either way."

"Key," I said.

Mixon pulled a set of keys from his pocket and said, "I assume you're simply going to surprise your old friend and talk to him."

"I like that assumption," I said.

"And I like my job," said Mixon. "I don't want to go back to the multiplication tables in Fresno, if they'd even take me back."

"Key," I said.

"This is a decent hotel," Mixon said, looking around as if he'd never seen the lobby of the Carlton Arms before. "You can get a clean room for a buck a night, no questions asked."

"It's the Plaza of Los Angeles," I said. "Key."

Mixon nodded knowingly and hit the bell in front of him. A girl with freckles and a maroon uniform with polished-brass buttons appeared and looked for my luggage.

"Connie," Mixon said. "Please let Mr. Peters into room 342. He's an old friend of Mr. Spelling's."

Connie smiled, showing large dazzling-white teeth, and took the offered passkey from Mixon. I nodded to Mixon and followed the bouncing Connie, who hurried across the lobby. The sleeping old man in the rumpled brown suit seemed to sense us coming, opened his eyes again, gave me a look of disgust, and tried to lift himself from the chair.

"Noise," he grumbled. "How can a man rest with . . ."

He waved his arms around and sank back, staring across the lobby at a painting on the wall of a young woman filling a pitcher with water at an outdoor fountain.

"Mr. Walters," Connie said, nodding at the old man. "Used to be a movie writer. Bronco Billy Anderson, even Chaplin. Long before my time. Talks a lot about somebody named John Bunny. Elevator or stairs?"

"Up to you," I said.

She nodded brightly and started up the carpeted stairs, bounding with energy. I wanted her to slow down, but I didn't want to tell her. So I did my best to bound.

She waved and said hello to a naval officer and a woman with him old enough to be his wife. She greeted an overly made-up old woman dressed in a draping gossamer which was more appropriate for Cairo in 1914 than Los Angeles in 1943.

"Mrs. Forbes-Hughes," said Connie over her shoulder, bounding ever upward. "You look great today."

"Thank you," Mrs. Forbes-Hughes of ancient Egypt said to Connie.

"Third floor," Connie announced as I came up the last four steps and stood at her side, trying not to breathe heavily.

"Are you always like this?" I asked, panting and trying not to show it, which is not easy.

"Like what?" she said, striding down the hall.

"Like one of those birds in *Snow White*. Katharine Hepburn in *Bringing Up Baby*."

"Movies," she said, nodding in understanding as she strode on. "My mom told me when I was four to keep positive, keep moving, keep my eyes open, and always, always smile in public and have a good word for everyone."

"Must take a lot out of you," I said as we stopped in front of 342.

"I'm still young," she said. "Nineteen in April. I figure if I can keep a positive attitude till I'm twenty-one, it'll be natural and I won't have to work so hard at it."

"Must make your parents proud," I said, waiting for Connie to open the door.

"Dad died last year. Rabaul."

"Sorry," I said.

"Thank you," she said, opening the door. "How much did you pay Sandy?"

I stepped in. Her voice had been bright, alive.

"I . . ."

"Doesn't matter," she said, holding up a hand and looking around the room. "It was more than you had to pay. Sandy is a talker. Can't stop talking. You want him to tell you something, just wait. If you outlast him, you don't have to pay him."

"Fifteen dollars," I said, looking at the tired furniture.

"I don't make that in a week," she said, moving to the door. I fished out another five and held it out.

"Nope," she said. "Make it two if you have change. If you don't, I do. I'm not out to cheat you, just make an honest living and enough to go to U.S.C. next year."

I found two singles and gave them to her.

"You know Spelling? The guy in this room."

"Can't get a smile out of him," Connie said, tucking the singles into her pocket. "Not bad looking. If he made a pass, I wouldn't fumble, but I'd have to get a smile out of him first."

"Maybe I can make him smile when he gets back," I said, moving to the armchair near the window and turning it so it faced the door.

"I don't think I like the way you just said that," she said. "You're a bill collector?"

"Something like that," I said. "He owes a dentist for some work."

"You have a son?" she asked, standing in the doorway.

"No," I said sitting. "Why?"

"Don't know," she said with a shrug. "You're kinda cute for an older guy. I wondered if there was one at home like you, only younger."

"Home is a single room in a boardinghouse on Heliotrope," I said, closing my eyes. "There's a cat there named Dash, a Swiss translator three feet tall, and a deaf landlady."

"You want to meet my mother? She's a widow."

"I know," I said. "I'll let you know."

"She's a fine-looking lady," Connie said. "Younger than you, I think. She has spunk like me."

"I don't know how much spunk I can take, Connie," I said.

"Am I too much?" she said with a grin full of white teeth.

"Not in small doses."

"He usually gets home about three or four," she said. "Then he goes out again, maybe at six-thirty, in the soup and fish till late, long after I've gone home. My mother's a great cook. Greek."

"Thanks, Connie," I said.

"Think about my mother," she said on her way out.

"How do you know I'm not a bluebeard who'll love your mother, take her money, and chop her head off?"

"You're a pussycat," she said, closing the door.

I sat for about two minutes in depression, an old guy with no sense of humor, no son, no wife, and too weary to meet a woman with spunk. Depression. Then I started to think about Tools Nathanson. How had he found Victor Spelling before I did? Tools didn't strike me as graduate-school material. Yet he had tracked down his boss's or partner's killer without the help of Mame Stoltz at M-G-M or Sheldon Minck's patient file.

I took my .38 from my shoulder holster, opened it, and checked to be sure the bullets weren't rusty. I almost never use it and I never remove the bullets. I could lie and say I kept them in at all times because I never knew when I might need some protection. The truth was I was too lazy to remove the bullets when I wasn't using the gun.

I searched Victor Spelling's room. It didn't take long. He kept little there—clothes in the closet, toothbrush and green Teel, a razor, some magazines. No notes, no diary, no letters.

There was a crumpled *L.A. Times* on the night table next to the bed. I picked it up as I sat again. If Spelling kept the schedule Connie reported, I had a few hours.

In the next twenty minutes, I learned from Hedda Hopper that Cole Porter's *Let's Face It!* might be coming to Los Angeles with Jose Ferrer and Vivian Vance, that there was a one-dollar dinner special with charcoal broil at the Pixie on LaBrea, that Mohandas K. Gandhi was in the eighteenth day of a planned twenty-one-day fast to obtain his unconditional release from internment at Poona, that Nazi puppet authorities in the protectorate of Bohemia and Moravia were threatening the Czechs with ever-harsher punishments if they didn't cooperate more fully with the anti-Allied war effort, that Congressman Will Rogers, Jr., would match wits tonight on "Information Please" with Clifton Fadiman, Oscar Levant, John Kiernan, and Franklin P. Adams.

Footsteps were coming down the corridor outside of room 342. I dropped the newspaper when the steps stopped in front of the door across from me. I took out my .38 and held it in my lap. Someone fiddled with the door and it popped open.

"I was just thinking about you," I said, holding up the .38 where Tools Nathanson could see it.

He stood surprised in the open doorway, his jacket open, a thin screwdriver in his hand. He looked at me for an instant and thought. I figured he was wondering about simply closing the door and getting the hell out of there, but there was something else on his mind. He stepped in, closed the door, and put his little screwdriver back in his tool belt.

"You set Karl up," Tools said, taking a step toward me. He was wearing a pair of brown trousers, a black sweater, and a sport jacket that almost matched the sweater but was no match for the trousers.

"Have a seat. We'll talk about it while we wait for Spelling."

Tools clanked two steps toward me and pointed his pudgy finger toward my face.

"You set Karl up. Came in with that bull-shit story while your pal Spelling waited for Karl to step out."

"That's stupid, Tools," I said with an intolerant sigh.

"Stupid? I follow you and find you in his room a couple of

hours after Karl was blown to pieces, sitting there, waiting for him."

He took another step toward me. I leveled the pistol at his face. He waved it off.

"You're not shooting me," he said. "Not if you're tellin' the truth about this Spelling. And if you ain't, you'll shoot anyway."

He was right. I put the pistol back in my holster and folded my arms.

Tools sat next to me.

"I want him to come through the door. I want to nail the son of a bitch to the wall, file his fingers to the bone, screw his kneecaps together, and staple his eyes shut," Tools said, taking a large pliers from his tool belt. "Start, now. Tell me what's going on."

I started. I went over everything, told him about my contact at M-G-M, how I got where I was standing. Then I sat back and watched his face as he tried to understand what he had just been told.

"Because of Karl's initials?" he finally said. "You think Spelling killed him because his initials fit? His life didn't mean anything but the name his old man gave him?"

"Maybe," I said. "Or maybe Karl just happened to be in the wrong movie at the wrong time."

Tools shifted on the sofa, looked at me as if he might see something that would make more sense than he was hearing.

"What're you, nuts?" he said, leaning over to poke me with a stubby finger. "I'll tell you how I found Spelling."

The door came open. I hadn't heard footsteps, a key in the lock. Spelling was standing there, black trousers, a white shirt with short sleeves, a look on his face like a startled animal.

I went for my gun. Tools got to his feet. Spelling fumbled in his pocket. Before Spelling could get his hand out of his pocket, Tools was lumbering toward him. Spelling took a step back into the hall. I was out of my chair by now, but it didn't do me much good. Spelling kicked the attacking Tools right in the face with his dark oxfords. Tools staggered back into my arms. Tools had something in his hand, a screwdriver. I tried to hold him. I couldn't. Spelling's eyes met mine and he grinned as Tools charged again. Now Spelling had a gun in his hand. The hell with it. I aimed my .38 in Spelling's general direction. Spelling fired once. The bullet cracked the ceiling. I took a shot at Spelling's head as Tools tackled him. I missed. Spelling fired again as Tools, sitting on his chest, brought the screwdriver up. The shot hit Tools's chest and came out on the other side, moving toward me. I was diving behind the sofa.

Two more shots ripped through the sofa near my face. I went down flat. Two more bullets, lower. Both were close. He could have climbed over the sofa, firing. He might have landed on my head.

"The grove," Spelling cried out.

The hell with it again. I stood up, gun leveled as Spelling ran through the open apartment door. I shot, but he was out of sight. I hurried past Tools's body and stepped into the corridor. Spelling was almost at the stairwell. He turned toward me, weapon aimed at my face.

"Too much left to do," he said. "I liked you when we started, but you're beginning to irritate me, Peters."

I took another shot at Spelling. It crashed into plaster right next to the elevator and he darted down the stairs. I went after him. He was almost to lobby level. I moved as fast as I could and missed him when I got there.

I looked at Mixon behind the hotel desk.

"Which way?" I asked.

"Who? Spelling? No way. He just went up to his room three, four minutes ago."

The sleeping old man who wrote movies for the likes of Bronco Billy shouted, "Goddamn it all. A man pays his rent.

A man deserves to rest." He looked at me, saw the gun in my hand, and said, "That does it."

I turned around and next to the elevator found the stairs to the basement.

"Call the cops," I yelled over my shoulder. "And an ambulance. Guy's hurt in Spelling's room."

"Oh, shit," Mixon moaned behind me.

The stairway down to the basement was dark, narrow, and bore no connection to gracious living. Something banged ahead of me. I plunged down by the light of the low-watt bulbs and found myself in the basement, the dark basement.

"Spelling?" I said.

No answer.

"Spelling," I repeated, stepping forward, gun held high. "Come on out. We'll talk."

"Nothing to say," Spelling's voice came from who knows where.

I stepped forward on my toes, moving toward where I thought the voice might have come from.

"Clark Gable," I reminded him.

No answer. The sound of a breaking window. I hurried forward or at least deeper into the darkness.

"Got a father, Peters?" his voice and the shot of a gun rang out.

I stopped, got on my knees, and groped for the wall.

"I had a father," I said.

"Everybody had a father," Spelling's voice echoed. "What about now?"

"Father's dead," I said, inching my way toward his voice along the wall.

"Gable killed my father," he whispered. "And I intend to make him pay. Make you all pay."

"How did he kill your father?" I asked.

"Look at the pictures," he said, even more quietly than before.

"If you . . ." I began but I stopped when I heard the sound of broken glass crushed underfoot. By the time I found the window, Spelling was gone.

I put my .38 away and made my way back up to the third floor, not letting my eyes meet Mixon's when I went through the lobby.

"Police are on the way," he called as I ran up the stairs.

Connie the bellhop was leaning over the fallen Tools Nathanson. She looked up at me, a hopeful smile on her face.

"I think he's alive," she said.

"Good," I said, breathing hard.

"Did you shoot him?" she asked.

"No," I said.

"He's a carpenter or something," Connie said.

"Something," I said, looking down at Tools, whose eyelids were fluttering.

"You'll be fine," Connie said cheerfully to Tools, who coughed, sputtered, opened his eyes, and looked around. He saw me and held out his hand. I took it. He tried to speak. Tools wheezed so softly that I had to get down on one knee to be sure he had said what I thought he said. He grabbed my shirt and pulled me down with more strength than a dying man should have. My head almost hit Connie's.

"I want you should get that bastard," Tools gasped. "Karl was the goods. Do it for Karl or I'll pull your kidneys out with a hacksaw and a number-five mechanic's pliers."

"Number five," I repeated.

"Mechanic's pliers," Tools whispered, letting go of my shirt as his eyes began to close again.

"I think . . ." Connie began and Tools came to life again, saying: "Nail him, Peters."

"I'll nail him, Tools," I said. "I'm a sucker for sentimental appeals."

"I've got a brother," Tools went on. "His name is . . . is . . . can't remember. Oh, Ronald. Accountant in Cleveland. Ronald Nathanson."

Two pair of feet crashing down the corridor. I looked up. Uniformed cops in the doorway. Both my age or older. Both with guns in their hands.

"Show your hands," the first cop said.

I showed my hands.

"You too," said Cop Two.

Connie showed her hands.

"Is he dead?" said the first cop, leaning toward Tools, ready to shoot him again if he suddenly leapt into the air in spite of the hole in his chest.

"Not yet," I said, standing up and helping Connie to her feet.

The first cop was thin with yellow drinker's eyes. The second cop looked like a milk carton with a sad face mounted on top.

"Will one of you call the Wilshire District and tell Captain Pevsner I've got some answers?"

"You a police officer?" Cop One asked.

"Something like that," Connie answered, looking down at Tools with deep concern. "Collection agency."

"You shoot this guy?" Cop Two asked, looking down at Tools's very pale face.

"No," I said as he patted me down, found my gun, removed it, smelled the barrel.

"Gun's just been fired," Cop Two said.

"At the guy who did this," I explained. "His name's Spelling. He killed three people in the last week. If the ambulance doesn't get here soon, it's going to be four people."

"I think he'll be fine," Connie said hopefully.

The cops didn't answer.

"You both married?" she asked.

The cops looked at each other and then at me.

"Her mother's a widow," I explained.

Tools gave out a sound like air escaping from a balloon. We all looked at him.

"Got a picture of your mother?" Cop Two asked.

"No, but there's one in my purse," Connie said brightly. "Down in the hotel locker room. I can run down and get it."

"You do that, miss," Cop Two said.

Connie looked at me, at Tools, and at the two cops before she went through the door.

"Spunky," Cop Two said.

"Just the word I'd use," I said.

"Let's sit down and wait," said Cop One.

And we did.

Chapter 10

The Melody Lounge on Main was almost empty when Phil and I got there. It was early afternoon. The drunks had mostly slid away for a few hours to try to give the impression that they had something to do besides drink in a dark bar where the ceiling fan whined like an engine trying to rev up. The soldiers, sailors, and marines hadn't started their evening yet and the businessmen and women from the neighborhood were still sitting in their offices, watching the clock and listening to Duke Ellington's version of "C Jam Blues."

I had been escorted to Phil's office by two silent cops, and Phil had listened quietly to my story.

"So," I had concluded, talking fast. "The way I see it, Spelling is out for revenge for something that happened to his father."

"And," Phil had said, touching his forehead to be sure it was still sweating, "you think his father may have been shish-kebabed with a sword while Atlanta burned?"

"Something like that," I said.

Phil had nodded.

"Security records were destroyed at Selznick," I said, "but the security guy on duty that night was Wally Hospodar."

"Jolly Jowly Hospodar?" asked Phil. "Used to work prostitution on the beaches?"

"Same," I had said. "I'm planning to hit the bar where he hangs out and see what he remembers. You checked with Culver City Police about the guy who caught the sword in his stomach in '38?"

"John Doe," said Phil. "Suspicious accident. No witnesses. Short report. Busy season. Case closed."

"Let's go see Wally Hospodar and open it again," I said.

Phil had folded his hands and put his thick white knuckles to his lips. I sat quietly waiting, fighting the almost irresistible urge to prod him with the right word.

"Let's go," he finally said, standing up.

And we went.

Now we were in the Melody Lounge in search of what had once been Wally Hospodar. We found him on the last bar stool in the corner, biting his lower lip and looking off into mirrors inside of mirrors, trying to remember something or someone. Phil and I sat on either side of him. He looked at us in the mirror and we looked at him. He was ruddy-faced and long past jowly.

"That clarinet," Wally said. "Barney Bigard. Ellington's a goddamn genius. G-C, sol-do, variations. That trombone, right there? Tricky Sam Nanton. You missed Ray Nance's opening violin solo."

"You know a lot about music," I said.

"I know a lot about sitting here," Wally said, looking up at us in the mirror behind the bar.

"The brothers Pevsner," he went on, finishing a whiskey and reaching for a bottle of beer. "You each take a round if I perform magic and tell you why you're here?"

"I'll take two rounds, Wally," I said, waving to the bartender, who was rinsing out some mugs for me and Phil. We looked like the beer type.

"Fine," said Wally. "You want to know about the guy who died that night in '38 at Selznick."

"You got it," Phil said impatiently.

Wally smiled at his empty and sucked his teeth.

"Knew it. Angelina said some guy called, fishing around about me, the night the guy got killed."

"He say anything else to Angelina?" Phil asked, waving away the barkeep and refusing a drink after Wally had his refill.

"Not so's she'd tell me. I met Angelina in Fort Worth."

"That a fact?" Phil said.

"I'll have a beer, draft, whatever you've got," I said to the waiting bartender, who clopped away.

Wally was looking into an eternity of mirrors, moving away from the Melody Lounge, from here and now. He was well on his way to being lost in dreams of Fort Worth.

The song on the jukebox ended.

"Angelina says she loves you and doesn't want you to come home."

"I'll drink to that," he said, draining his glass and pointing to his empty as the bartender, a lanky cowboy in boots, clopped back in our direction. "And plenty more where that came from."

"Maybe not," the barkeep said, glumly picking up Wally's glass. "You know the War Production Board just made eighty alcohol plants switch from the drinking stuff to industrial?"

"I knew that," I said, turning to Wally, but the bartender, who needed some Sen-Sen, a shave, and a better sense of timing, went on.

"And the Woman's Christian Temperance Union met a month or so back in Birmingham, more than a thousand of them. And you know what they want?"

I could see Phil's fists clenching just below bar level.

"What?" I asked.

"Total prohibition again," the bartender said. "Through the war and after."

"Never happen," Wally said.

"Listen," the bartender said, pulling a folded newspaper clipping from the pocket of his plaid shirt.

"You," Phil said, putting his hands palm-down on the bar, a very, very bad sign.

"Just take a second," the bartender said, ignoring Phil and unfolding the clipping to read. "This was what the president of the W.C.T.U. said. Her name's Ida B. Wise Smith. Listen. 'There is hardly an activity of the home front of more importance to the American cause. Liquor is our most widespread and dangerous saboteur, and it is our patriotic duty to halt its ravaging of manpower, material, resources and physical stamina.' "

The bartender looked at us as he stuffed the clipping back in his pocket. "Nothing in there," he said, "about the time and work wasted, or the trains and buses and cars wasting gas and tires to get to Alabama."

"Trains don't have tires," Wally said.

"I was just lumping," the bartender said with a shrug. "It's the point, not the details, if you know what I mean."

"I know what you mean," I said.

"Get the man his drink," Phil said, doing his best to contain himself.

The bartender gave Phil a sneer, turned, and went for the bottle.

Music suddenly drummed through the floor. A woman of the afternoon in a red dress and a bad mood was giving us an I-dare-you look and swaying to the opening notes of "Tangerine."

"What was in the report, Wally?" I asked as the bartender came back with my beer.

"Turn off the jukebox," Phil said, rubbing his gray hair with the palm of his hand. A very bad sign.

"Lady's got a right," the bartender said with a shrug.

"Then turn it down," Phil said as the bartender turned away.

The bartender just walked and the music rose. It seemed to be pushing Wally into alcoholics' dreamland. Phil got off his stool and strode toward the lady in red, who gave him a knowing smile and held up her arms, waiting to dance. Phil walked past her and kicked the jukebox right in the speaker. It groaned and shut up.

"What the? . . ." the woman screamed.

"Hey, asshole," the lanky bartender shouted, coming over the bar with a sawed-off bat in his hand.

"It was on fire," Phil said. "I just saved your bar. You owe me one."

The bartender was moving on Phil, who started back toward his stool next to us.

"Stop there," Phil said, holding up a hand. "I'm a police officer and I'm in one lousy mood. You want your nose smashed as flat as my brother's over there, just keep coming."

The bartender threw the bat in the general direction of my brother, but it was so wide and to the right that it had to be a pickoff play or a wild pitch to save face.

"He really a cop?" the woman in red screamed at me.

"Yep," I said.

"Let's get out of here," Phil said. "Before I do something I won't regret."

I dropped another one of Clark Gable's five-spots. When the bartender glared at me, I dropped another five to ease his pain.

"Get out of here," the bartender said softly through clenched teeth, in a not-bad Gary Cooper.

Normally, that would have been enough to insure Phil's staying around to do some real personal and property damage.

But I was off the stool now and ushering Wally toward the door. The lady in red went into the sunlight just ahead of us as we passed in front of Phil, now glowering at the barkeep.

"I don't want him in here for a month," the bartender said, pointing at Wally. "A month. He's trouble and you're it."

Phil shook his head and joined me and Wally as we went through the Melody Lounge door and onto Main Street. A rain was coming and the lady in red was disappearing into a bar across the street. Nobody paid much attention to us, either because they had seen falling-down drunks before or they had enough instinct to recognize that the hefty guy with the marine haircut was waiting for an excuse.

"What was that?" I asked, leading Wally toward Phil's car.

"Soliciting to commit prostitution. Creating a public nuisance. Catching me when I'm in a bad mood. Hospodar," he said as I set Wally gently down on the fender, "what was in that damn report? Have we got conspiracy to cover a possible murder or what?"

Wally's clothes, now that I could see them in the sunlight, were clean and neat. He was shaved and his hair cut. He was holding onto something he had been, but his grip was loose.

"Made a mistake," Wally mumbled. "One day a decision had to be made and I'd long lost the ability or desire to decide. I didn't step in when two execs were fighting about something, and one of them broke the other guy's face when I was two feet away. Guy with the broken face was a cousin of Louis B.'s wife. End of career."

"I'm sorry," I said.

"And I'm running out of patience," Phil said.

Wally took a deep breath, let it out, and shook like a dog coming out of water.

"No cover-up," he said. "Went through Culver City Police. County attorney's office said it was probably an accident. Dead guy with the sword in his chest was one S. P. Ling . . ."

"Spelling," I said.

". . . who had outstanding warrants in three states," Wally went on. "Pennsylvania, Ohio, and New York. Two were felonies, one for attempted murder. He did time on an armed robbery when he was a kid. Got the acting bug in prison. S. P. Ling, Actor Ling. Aliases included Sid Spelling and . . . I forget."

Wally was reaching for something in his empty shirt pocket. He managed to get two fingers in the pocket and came up empty.

"And the records were burned?" I asked.

"Fried," said Wally. "Fire of suspicious origin. Lots of people out there with grudges."

"Maybe someone who wanted the Ling file burned," I said.

"What the hell for?" Phil came in impatiently.

"I had some thoughts on that one," said Wally. "Kept 'em to myself though."

"Get in the car," Phil said. "We'll sober you up and talk about it when you get out of the drunk tank tomorrow."

"He's doing fine, Phil," I said.

"I'm not doing fine," Phil said, thumbing himself on the chest. "Get him in the car. Now."

We were wedged against the curb, so we walked into the street and I opened the rear door as Phil climbed into the driver's seat. Cars were passing going both ways, so I didn't hold the door open all the way. I wouldn't have looked up at all if the car that was coming at us hadn't burned rubber with a screeching start, definitely an unpatriotic move during a rubber shortage. I still wouldn't have paid much attention if I hadn't looked up to see the car roaring toward us and Spelling, Jr., in the driver's seat. I pushed the dazed Wally into the back seat and tried to dive onto the top of Phil's car. I almost made it. Spelling missed me by a deep sigh and plowed into the open door. The door and Spelling exploded down Main Street. I turned my head and watched the car door spinning in the air. It missed the head of a mailman by about a foot and crashed through the window of a tailor shop, sending glass raining into the street, where people covered their heads and screamed.

"You all right?" Phil said as I slid back to the street on shaking legs.

"Yeah, I think so," I said.

"Then get your ass in here," shouted Phil. "I'm gonna catch that son of a bitch."

I threw myself into the car as Phil pulled onto Main, scraping the rear fender of the Ford sedan in front of us and almost hitting a green Tudor Chevy that hit its brakes just in time.

"Wally?" I said, but Wally had passed out.

We were going fast on a busy city street. I didn't want to know how fast. Phil wasn't talking. He turned on the radio and Claude Thornhill's record of "Where Oh Where Has My Little Dog Gone?" blared out. Five minutes earlier, music had driven him over the edge. Now he was fueled by it. All bad signs. I shut up and sat on Wally Hospodar on the floor of the back seat.

"That was Spelling," I said over the music.

Phil didn't answer.

"I think he's the son of the guy who died," I went on. "I wonder why he wanted to kill Wally?"

Phil laughed.

"I saw him coming in the rearview," shouted Phil. "You dumb shit. He was after you."

"Right," I said. "Can't you go any faster?"

He tried. Through lights and past scurrying pedestrians. Across a sidewalk or two and through narrow alleys. Phil could have called for help on his radio, but he sang along with the music and hit the floorboard, which would have troubled me less if my brother hadn't been singing between his teeth in German.

"*Zu Lauterbach hab ich mein Strump verloren,*" Phil sang. "That's the way the huns sang it."

Spelling went out of control near the park. His car went into a spin, bounced off a lamp post, and almost rolled over. Phil hit the brake and skidded to a stop next to a fire hydrant upon which a man in a Panama hat was tying his shoe. When we came out of the three-door car, the man in the Panama was shaking and Spelling was out of his car and on his way. He could run. I couldn't and neither could Phil. Not like that. Even when we were kids.

"Get back in the car," Phil shouted.

I got back in, knowing we weren't going to catch him now. We'd circle the park, but Spelling would go out wherever he wanted, maybe even double back. Phil knew it too, but he wouldn't admit it even to himself.

We went around the park, watching for a sign of Spelling. Nothing. We went around again and then tried streets off of the park. Some of them three times.

Suddenly, Phil turned off the radio and parked next to the Tail of the Pup hot-dog stand. Normally, Phil was a sucker for their kosher dogs. He pounded on the steering wheel with his fists for about a minute and then said, "You want a burger?"

"Hot dog, if it's a kosher," I said.

Nobody moved. Not Phil, who shut his eyes. Not me. Definitely not Wally Hospodar, who, for all I knew, was dead.

"What are we doing, Phil?" I finally asked.

"I'm meditating," he said calmly. "It doesn't do any goddamn good, but I'm meditating."

After three or four minutes, Phil took a deep breath, opened his eyes, and used his car radio to call for someone to come for Spelling's wrecked car.

"And I want Loring to go over it. No one else. Loring. You get that? Anyone touches anything on the car but Loring gets his lower lip ripped off."

Phil signed off, hung up the radio, and stared out of the front window.

I had some ideas, but I knew better than to say anything. A good sigh later, Phil said, "I'll put a man on Hospodar and one on Varney," he said. "You?"

"Let's just catch him," I said.

"Just get me a double burger," Phil said, climbing out of the car.

"You want mustard, onion, and pickles?" I said, stepping out of the hole where there had recently been a door.

Phil nodded and reached for his wallet as we walked toward the Pup.

I stopped him with, "This one's on Clark Gable."

We had finished our sandwiches—mine was a Colossal dog with coleslaw instead of kraut—before we discovered that Wally Hospodar was dead.

Actually, I discovered that Wally was dead when I offered him the regular dog with chili and he fell on his face. There was a hole in his back, a thin hole. My guess was that he was passed out when he died. Phil was sitting in the driver's seat when I told him Wally was dead. Phil snatched the chili dog out of my hand and downed it in three angry bites.

"How could Spelling get back to the car before us when we were on his damn ass?" Phil sputtered through a mouthful of mustard and bun.

"I don't know, Phil," I said, still standing outside the car next to him and watching the traffic flow by.

"And how the hell do I explain stopping for lunch with a corpse in the back seat, a dead man killed in my own car?"

"I don't know, Phil."

"Damn," Phil said, hitting the steering wheel. "Get in."

"I think I'll . . ."

"Get the hell in the car," Phil said, tearing at his tie.

I got in.

Chapter 11

I had a headache. Mrs. Plaut fixed a bag of her Aunt Ginger's Yellow Indian Poultice, which she instructed me to apply to the cut on my forehead. Mrs. Plaut also gave me a Boxie Scotch Bromide, yellow crystals dissolved in water, which I was instructed to "drink down without pause or risk dyspepsia."

The price I had to pay for poultice and bromide, which had not yet kicked in, was to read another chapter of Mrs. P's never-ending history of her family.

It all began when Mrs. Plaut first rented a room to me, a little over two years ago. For reasons still unclear to me, which Gunther suggested I not explore, Mrs. Plaut believed I was either an exterminator or a book editor, possibly both. So far she hadn't asked me to get rid of the ants, crickets, or funny-looking green things with wings that sometimes got in the house. These she disposed of with her own remedies and frequent applications. No, she turned to me for help with the history of the family Plaut.

I had read more than a thousand pages, written in Mrs. Plaut's neat block letters on lined sheets. The new batch, which she handed me with the poultice and the bromide concoction and more information on changes in the ration-book regulations, was mercifully short.

I couldn't complain. Mrs. Plaut had agreed to let me hold a meeting in the all-day-and-early-evening room, a big fire-placed room with a faded Navajo rug which was reserved for "quiet" moments and "music listening" time for the roomers. The room was seldom used by anyone but Mr. Hill the mail-man, who sometimes paused to take off his shoes and rest his feet before pulling himself up the stairs. Mr. Hill, in full gray uniform, was known to doze off snoring, clutching his empty leather mailbag to his chest. Once in a while, Mrs. Plaut would come in serious or beaming to wind the Victrola and play such favorites as "Hindustan," "Indian Love Call," "Juntos en El Rincon," and "After You've Gone." Most of the records were so old they were recorded on one side only. Most were by Isham Jones and his band, though there were a few Ted Lewis and King Olivers in the scratchy pile.

My headache, the yellow poultice, and I lay on the mattress on the floor going through the pages Mrs. Plaut had handed me. I read:

> My brother Bill and his friends Murryhill and Weston were to have charged up San Juan Hill astride their horses right behind Teddy Roosevelt himself. Weston later claimed that Blackjack Pershing was also among their elite company, but Brother was certain that Pershing's brother was back at camp tending the backup horses.
>
> Well, anyway, Brother, Murryhill, and Weston assembled on horseback and followed a contingent they thought was the first wave of cavalry. It turned out, as you may have sur-mised from small hints I have given you, that they were in-correct. Brother Bill always contended, to the day he died in Mineola, that Colonel Roosevelt had not been entirely clear on time or location of assembly.

There is, however, no point in contemplating what can not have been.

Bill Murryhill, who was quite bald and had been since early childhood from what was reputed to be a misapplication to the scalp of Mrs. Tessmacher's Panacea in a Bottle, and Weston lost no time in urging their steeds to the fore and upon seeing a lone rider charge at a gallop up a ridge, Brother opined that it was Teddy and he urged Murryhill and Weston, who had but one eye due to an ice cream machine accident in Toledo, to gallop on to glory with the first wave Rough Riders in their moment of triumph.

When they reached the crest of the hill with no resistance from the enemy who they were convinced had fled at the fearsome sight of determined American cavalry, they looked around for Teddy and back for the rest of the Riders. Of Riders there appeared to be none. Of Teddy, they had been mistaken. The man on the horse, who was no longer on the horse, was sitting with legs crossed on the grass and holding his head. His name was Tom Mix. He had a winning smile and an enormous nose and would go on to greater fame as a movie star and circus curiosity.

Tom Mix had been carried away by the horse he had been breaking, a Roan of ill disposition who now stood munching grass and looking at the small group. Tom Mix had sustained a bump on his head.

At that moment, so Brother recalled, there was a tremendous whooping and hollering from the hill to their right veiled by thick trees. As they discovered subsequently, it was the Battle of San Juan Hill.

The contingent, Tom Mix, Murryhill, and Weston, led by Brother Bill went down the far side of the hill leading their exhausted horses and found themselves in a small town called Rosalinda where the populace greeted them without enthusiasm as liberators from the Spanish yoke.

Though Tom Mix claimed to speak fluent Spanish, it turned out that he knew only enough words to get himself in trouble. Remember, however, that he was a young lad at the time and full of suds.

Weston, however, knew enough to announce a fiesta of victory over Spain and a great party was held that evening albeit there was little to eat and drink. Murryhill did not return with Brother, Tom Mix, and Weston the next morning. He fell in with a family named Calles taking up with either the daughter or aunt of the family, Weston's Spanish being too poor to determine which.

Brother Bill reported that Murryhill had died in the charge and he was backed up in this deceit by Tom Mix and Weston. Murryhill became a hero of the charge on San Juan Hill and a statue was erected in his memory in downtown Enid, Oklahoma where he was from. Subsequently, Tom Mix visited Enid and made a fine speech about his partner Murryhill. A children's park in Enid was named in honor of Murryhill. I know not if it still stands but I understand on good authority that it contained the first twenty-foot children's slide in either Oklahoma or Texas.

Weston became a bartender in Florida somewhere along the Suwanee River and Brother married a harness maker's daughter and moved to Healdsburg in the Californias where he repaired typewriters and telegraphs and wrote many a newspaper article about his exploits with the Rough Riders.

There was more, much more, but not for me. Not today. I closed my eyes and opened them almost immediately. Mrs. Plaut was standing in my doorway, arms folded, wearing a yellow dress with a print of large red flowers and a straw hat with a wide brim.

"They are assembled," she said.

She had something in her hand. I blinked. It was a small garden shovel covered with dirt.

"You've been reading," she said, pointing the shovel at the pile of papers.

"And you've been planting," I countered with aplomb.

"A garden is a lovesome thing," she said, returning her shovel to parade-dress military position.

"I'll remember that," I said, sitting up. "Now if you'll . . ."

"I'm going downstairs," she said, taking the yellow poultice from my hand. "I'm brewing some hot mixed-berry saft and there is many an orange snail muffin remaining. Have you finished reading about Brother in Puerto Rico?"

"I have," I said. "Murryhill was an interesting character."

Mrs. Plaut sighed and looked toward my window.

"I would have considered a marriage offer from him had he but importuned," she said. "Instead, Fatty Arbuckle and the Mister."

"Fatty Arbuckle?"

But she had turned her back and exited. I got up, arranged Mrs. Plaut's manuscript on my little kitchen table, and put a box of dominoes on the pile. I had my pants and shoes on and was considering whether to wear the clean white shirt with the missing button, the not-so-clean blue shirt with the small salsa stain, or the fashionable off-white with the unfashionably frayed collar. I took the off-white and was buttoning it when Dash leaped through the window.

"Wait'll I tell you about my day," I said.

Dash seemed interested, but I was in a hurry. I opened the cabinet over the small refrigerator in the corner near the window and pulled out a can of Strongheart dog food. I had picked up a dozen cans by mistake and discovered that Dash liked the stuff.

Over my shoulder I checked the Beech-Nut clock near the

door. Three-forty. I found the can opener while Dash sat back watching me.

"People are getting killed, Dash," I said.

Dash's pink tongue darted out and back while I poured the dog food into a bowl, tried not to smell it, and set it on the floor. Dash moved to the food and began eating.

"And killers are sending me poems about it."

Dash slurped away at the Strongheart.

"Will you answer a question for me?"

Dash paused to catch his breath. I took that for a yes. He went on eating.

"Is it too late for me to grow up? I'm asking you this because the loony who's writing these poems may want to kill me too. And, I ask you, what will I have left behind if he kills me? A cat, a few friends, no money, a Crosley that should be turned in for scrap metal."

Dash didn't care, but Mrs. Plaut, who had returned and opened the door without my hearing her, did have some ideas.

"First," she said, ignoring my yelp of surprise, "it is most assuredly too late for you to grow up for you have already done so. Second, I do not know what you will leave behind if Wendell Willke kills you. Actually, I think you must be seriously deluded to believe that Mr. Willke would have the slightest interest in you. But if you were to be hit by a Red Car on the Melrose line, I, though grieved, would request that one of your cronies take your cat."

"You are always a comfort to me in moments of indecision and self-doubt," I said.

"They are still waiting downstairs. They have consumed all of the remaining orange snail muffins, and the little fat one with the thick glasses and odious cigar has drunk one quart of saft and spilt another pint on the rug."

"I didn't invite Shelly," I said.

"And I hope you have not invited Keats or Byron," said

Mrs. Plaut. "I am playing the "Song of India" for those assembled, but while I am the gracious landlord, I always ask myself what the departed Mister would say in a situation."

"What would he say?" I said, buttoning my shirt.

"Tell them to keep their feet off the furniture, including the hassock, and that minimal refreshments will be served this day."

"I'm on the way down," I said.

"You said that once before," she said.

I took the box of dominoes off the manuscript, hoisted the tome in two hands, and handed it to her.

"Fascinating," I said.

"And all of it a factual chronicle," she said.

Far behind her, well beyond her doubtful hearing, someone shouted, then someone answered, then the shouting rose.

"I think we'd better get downstairs," I said, moving past her.

Dash dashed between my feet into the hallway, and Mrs. Plaut mumbled to herself that the age of chivalry had gone to rest with the Mister.

I went to the bathroom, brushed my teeth and hair, and looked at myself in the mirror. Mrs. Plaut's poultice was doing its job. The cut was clean, tight, small, and no longer discolored. I was ready for guests.

When I got to the day room, Shelly was standing in the center of the floor squinting through his bottle-bottom glasses at Gunther, who stood below him but didn't give an inch.

Jeremy sat on the sofa, arms folded, ignoring the confrontation and making notes on a pad. Next to him was Clark Gable, who sat, arms folded, shaking his head in disbelief. He was wearing a pair of worn khaki fatigue pants and an olive-colored long-sleeved shirt with a turtleneck.

Mame Stoltz sat on the Mister's rocking chair, reputed to have been the property of Mr. Abraham Lincoln's secretary of something or other. Mame was sleek, lean, hair short and dark, piled up to show her neck. She wore a gray blouse and matching skirt, with white pearls and plenty of makeup. She looked up when I came in and smiled.

"Toby," she said. "Landlady or no landlady, Clark and I are going to smoke."

Gunther and Shelly continued to glare at each other. Shelly made a low growling sound.

"Is that what they're fighting about?"

"They're fighting about someone named Mildred," Gable said, rubbing his forehead.

Without turning his gaze from Gunther, Shelly whined, "He made remarks about my wife."

"I said that Mrs. Minck bore no resemblance to Miss Stoltz," said Gunther, who looked at me seriously.

"Mildred is a Venus compared to her," Shelly said.

I glanced at Mame, who was playing with an unopened pack of Old Gold's.

"Mrs. Minck is of no anatomical distinction," Gunther insisted. "Physiological comparisons are of the most superficial kind."

I tended to agree with Gunther but I knew that folly and defeat lay in pursuing it with Sheldon, who had an unexplained loyalty to Mildred who vaguely resembled Marjorie Main on a bad day. Mildred had once run off with a Peter Lorre imitator and when he was dead returned to Shelly and took all the money the beachball of a dentist had hidden in an old vase.

"Shelly," I said, going for the idea that a strong offense would obscure the argument, "what are you doing here?"

This got his attention and he turned to me somewhat sheepishly while Gunther moved to Mame's side. Seated in the rocker, Mame was about the same height as Gunther, a mating made in Hollywood heaven.

"I heard that we were meeting. Jeremy said . . ."

"I did not," Jeremy said without looking up from his pad.

"Sit down, Shelly," I said.

"But that little . . ."

"Down, now, Sheldon," I said.

"I'm not apologizing," Shelly said, looking for a chair and finding a wooden one in the corner. "No. He'll apologize."

"Fine," I said, "let's . . ."

"But I will apologize to Mr. Gable," Shelly said, standing next to the chair.

"Apology accepted," Gable said with a smile and a glance at me that made it clear he was losing patience.

"In fact," Shelly said, as if he had a flash of inspiration, "I'll be glad to work on your teeth, cleaning, fillings, whatever, for half the celebrity price."

Mame whispered something to Gunther, who nodded.

"No, thank you," Gable said, pulling a cigarette from his pocket and putting it to his lips.

"But . . ." Shelly went on as Gunther moved quickly to his side and touched his arm. Shelly wanted to brush him away but Gunther insisted. Shelly sat in the wooden chair and Gunther whispered in his ear.

"No," said Shelly, looking at Gable, who looked as if he was seriously considering a run for the door. "Clark Gable? False teeth?"

"That's it," said Gable, rising. "Peters, I'm going out on the front porch with Mame. We are going to have a cigarette. When we are finished, I'm going home, where I will pack what few belongings I've brought to the States with me, and tomorrow I'll catch the first military air transportation I can find back to England. I'd like to get my hands on this Spelling, but there's a war going on and I think I'd better escape this . . ."

"Sideshow?" Mame suggested.

"I'll go with that," Gable said. "Five minutes."

He looked at his wristwatch and strode to the door with Mame a step behind him. Gunther stood blinking at the temporary loss of Mame to the call of tobacco and the company of Clark Gable.

"More saft?" Mrs. Plaut said amiably, coming into the room with a pitcher of dark liquid. "Iced this time."

I sat next to Jeremy in the spot Gable had been. No one answered Mrs. Plaut, who placed the pitcher on a wooden block on the coffee table.

"Thanks," I said.

"What happened to the lady and the man who looks like Robert Taylor?"

"Smoking on the front porch," I said, feeling that the businesslike atmosphere I had hoped for had vanished in smoke rings.

"I don't allow smoking in the house," Mrs. Plaut said, standing straight, smiling, and wiping her hands on the apron she had put on.

"We are painfully aware of that," I said.

"Not pipes or cigars," she said, looking at Shelly, who put his palms on his chest and squealed, "What did I do?"

"We've all done things about which we are not proud," Mrs. Plaut said. "You appear to have done more than the rest of us."

With that Mrs. Plaut departed.

"I haven't done anything," Shelly insisted, shoving his glasses back on his nose just as they were about to tumble into his lap.

"Violet Gonsenelli," I said, closing my eyes and regretting my words.

"Violet Gon . . . I haven't . . . she . . . I, we need a receptionist," Shelly said, pleading his case to the indifferent Jeremy and Gunther.

"That's it," I said, raising my voice. "That's it. People are dying out there. Some maniac may be trying to kill Clark Gable. Hell, he may be trying to kill me too. Let's, for God's sake, try to make some sense around here."

Gunther sat in the rocker. Shelly considered a rejoinder and changed his mind. Jeremy put his pencil in his pocket, folded his notebook, and said, "The police are watching Mr. Varney, who appears to be one of the final two remaining witnesses to the events that took place on the night Spelling's father died."

"Final two?" asked Shelly.

"I'm the other one," I said.

"Ah, good," said Shelly, sitting back with a satisfied smile.

"While we may assume that you are capable of defending yourself under reasonable circumstances," said Jeremy, "these circumstances are not reasonable and I suggest we take turns watching you from a discreet but alert distance."

Jeremy looked at each of us for comments. We had none, so he went on: "We have a series of poorly written poetic clues which present obscure hints to the identity of the next victim of Mr. Spelling."

"Ah ha," said Shelly.

Jeremy ignored him.

"Also present in these versified notes are allusions to a threat to Clark Gable, who has also been telephoned by the would-be poet," Jeremy said. "Couple this with the suggestion that something will take place, perhaps a final murder or two, where the stars meet tomorrow. Conclusion?"

"We're dealing with a nut," I said.

"Or we are dealing with a killer who is leading you someplace, Toby," Jeremy went on. "He is a step or two ahead of you, turning his head, luring you forth with a wave of the finger, a clue, a murder. Where is he leading you to, Toby? Where and why?"

"Jeremy, no offense, but we've got plenty of questions. What we need are answers," I said.

"The stars," Gunther said suddenly. "Under the stars. And what was it Juanita prophesied, the *grove*. The Academy Awards are being given tomorrow night at the Coconut Grove."

"Poetically appropriate," said Jeremy.

"I don't get it," said Shelly, pouring himself a fourth, fifth, or sixth glass of iced saft.

"Looks like our poet Spelling wants an audience for his next murder," I said. "He plans to kill someone at the Academy Awards dinner."

"It makes sense," said Jeremy.

"Who?" asked Shelly, ignoring the blue stain on his jacket from a dripping glass of saft. "Kill who? Why?"

"Lionel Varney," I said. "Varney'll be at the Academy Awards dinner."

"Then I suggest we say good-bye to Clark Gable, allow him to leave as he plans, and hope the police will do their job," Jeremy said, rising.

"I'll call Phil and tell him," I said.

"In case we are wrong, Toby," Gunther said, moving toward us as I stood, "may I suggest you remain as inconspicuous as possible."

"I'll go for a ride in the desert or catch a double feature," I said. "Or I . . ."

"I've got it," Shelly said, putting aside his glass of Mrs. Plaut's five-star saft and looking at us with a sappy smile. "Dental care for dentures. Special care of dentures for the stars. Discretion guaranteed. Newsletter on the latest denture research and inventions. I'll get a consultant. The Westmores. Well? What do you think?"

Neither Gunther nor Jeremy responded so I was stuck with humoring Shelly. "It has possibilities. Why don't you work out the details, put them on paper, see if there're any flaws, and then move ahead."

"No," Shelly said. "Inspiration. Came to me all at once. Perfect."

"Like your ideas for animal dentistry and tinted teeth," I said.

"Yeah, but even better," said Shelly. "Like, like I don't know. Magic. Maybe even God."

"If God is interested in such inspiration," said Jeremy seriously, "then he either has a sense of humor which is truly unfathomable, or free will is no longer a tenable concept."

"Yes," said Shelly gleefully. "You've got it."

"Shelly," I warned.

"Okay, okay, I'll discuss it with Mildred and Violet," he said, actually rubbing his chubby cigar-stained hands together. "Separately."

Gunther had hurried to the front porch, looking, I was sure, for Mame Stoltz before Clark Gable stole her heart away.

Jeremy stood silent, head cocked to one side until Shelly was finished and said, "Would you like me to stay with Gable tonight?"

"No," I said. "I'll do it. Maybe I can persuade him to join me at some desert motel or . . ."

Shelly was just standing there, working out the details, mumbling things like "It'll work" and "Low overhead. Maybe even work with Mark Marvel on the fourth floor. Therapy for celebrity denture-wearers. Learn to love your dentures."

Jeremy was holding out his hand to me. He opened it. There was a key in the massive palm.

"Van Nuys," he said. "Address is on the key. I'm remodeling the apartments, upgrading when I'm finished. That's the model. One bedroom. Everything including running water."

I took the key.

"Thanks, Jeremy," I said.

"I'll see you in the morning, Toby," Shelly said, waddling past us and into the afternoon.

"Alice would like to move," Jeremy said.

"Move?"

"To San Antonio. We both have relatives, and with the current market I can get a reasonable price for the Farraday and my other property and devote the remainder of my life to poetry."

"You can do that in Los Angeles," I said.

He shook his head and put a hand on my shoulder. "I cannot," he said. "Alice believes that you may eventually get me hurt or even killed. I've already committed one murder because of our association and . . ."

"That was an accident," I said in a whisper, looking around to be sure we hadn't been heard.

"I can deceive my mind but never my soul. Toby, Alice is right. We have Natasha. It would be nice if she had a father."

"I won't ask you for help anymore, Jeremy," I said, crossing my heart. "Promise."

"But I will offer or volunteer."

"I'll move out of the Farraday, other side of town. You can't really be thinking about leaving because of me."

"No," he said, removing his hand from my shoulder. "There are other reasons, private reasons. I've shared one public one with you, the one that touches our friendship. I'm not a young man."

"Saft?" said Mrs. Plaut, staggering into the day room with the weight of a fresh gallon of liquid in a pitcher balanced on a tray she was carrying.

Jeremy moved quickly to take the tray and place it on the table.

"Everyone's gone," she said, looking around.

"Miss Stoltz and the man who looks like Clark Gable are on the front porch smoking," I said.

Mrs. Plaut nodded knowingly.

"I think I put a touch too much gin in the saft," she said to us brightly.

"How much gin was in—?"

"One fifth to three-quarters of a gallon," she said. "Agnes Smeed's recipe. At least she was Agnes Smeed before she married Reed Clixco. I always thought it would be more interesting if he took her name when they married so he could be Reed Smeed, but, alas, that idea was long before its time which has not yet come except for the occasional suffragette and her passive concubine."

"I must be going, Toby," Jeremy said. "Perhaps I can catch Dr. Minck before he tries to drive. He drank at least a gallon of Mrs. Plaut's refreshing saft."

"We'll talk later, Jeremy," I said.

He nodded, shook Mrs. Plaut's hand, and went in search of Shelly.

"All in all a good tea party," Mrs. Plaut said, pouring herself a glass of saft.

"All in all," I agreed, pouring myself a glass.

"A toast, Mr. Peelers," Mrs. Plaut said, holding up her glass. "Absent friends."

"Absent friends," I repeated, touching my glass to hers.

I finished my glass at about the same time as Mrs. Plaut.

"It's the nectar that does it," she said.

"I'll help you clean up."

"Only one who I allowed to help with cleanup was the Mister."

I went through the day room into the hallway and onto the porch, where Mame Stoltz had already departed and Clark Gable was pacing and checking his watch.

"Sorry about that, Peters," he said. "In there, I mean."

"About what?"

"I got a little impatient. Hell, I lost all my patience, looked around and saw . . . some people trying to protect a man in uniform during a war. You've got to admit that you're relying on a quartet too old, small, or blind to be on active duty."

"Add lame," I said. "I'm both too old and I've got a bad back. You were right. We're a sideshow, but we're not half bad when the wind is blowing our way and the sun is shining."

"And the gods are looking down," said Gable with a smile.

I told him about our conclusion that Spelling would probably go for Lionel Varney at the Academy Awards the next night. It made sense to Gable. I told him that we might be wrong and that Spelling knew where Gable and I lived, so it might be a good idea for us to get out of L.A. for the night and for me to take him to whatever transportation back to England he might find on a Saturday.

"I don't hide, Peters," he said, sitting on the white porch railing.

"Why risk getting killed?" I said, leaning against the wall and watching a pair of smiling young women tooling down Heliotrope in a convertible. "Besides, the papers probably know you're back by now. They'll probably be waiting for you in Encino."

Gable shrugged and turned to see what I was looking at. The girl in the passenger seat looked up and saw him. She screamed and we could hear her squeal to the driver as they roared away.

"Clark Gable. I swear. On the porch. Go around the block. Really."

"I'm going home before they make it around the block, Peters," he said, getting up from the rail.

"They might spot you," I said.

"Naw, one of the nice things about a cycle is that you can wear a leather helmet and goggles and the police won't think you're about to rob a bank. Stay on the job and give me a call in the morning. I'll lock the doors and keep a gun next to my bed."

"I think you should . . ."

He was already down the stairs.

"Hitler's boys have been trying to shoot me out of the sky for almost a year," he said with a familiar lopsided grin. "His best haven't done it. I'm not about to let a stateside lunatic give the Fuehrer some good news."

I could hear the phone ringing inside the house. I couldn't tell if it was Mrs. Plaut's phone or the pay phone on the upstairs landing. Gable waved, a clipped little wave to the side, and hurried to his motorcycle parked at the curb. He was roaring down the street, head down, and went right past the girls in the convertible who had circled the block and were looking for the king. They paid no attention to the man on the motorcycle. I moved to the porch steps as the girls came up alongside the house.

"My friend says Clark Gable is on your porch," the driver shouted.

"He was," the passenger said.

"My cousin Conrad," I said. "Stunt man. Done some work for Gable."

"I could have sworn," said the passenger.

They both looked at me, a heavyset Chrysler waiting impatiently behind them for the girls to finish their conversation.

"Are you anybody?" the girl in the driver's seat said.

Her hair was long and black. Her skin perfect and tan. Her teeth as white as memory.

"No," I said. "I'm a plumber."

The guy in the Chrysler lost his patience and hit the horn. The girls drove off, away from the sunset and toward Sunset Boulevard.

"For you, Mr. Peelers," Mrs. Plaut said behind me. "Phone. Man from the brotherhood. Upstairs."

I thanked her and went back in the house, taking the stairs one at a time, feeling a little sorry for myself, determined to give Anne a call, a night out, some conversation, when Spelling was locked up. I picked up the phone. It was Phil.

"Can't give Varney any cover," he said abruptly.

"Can't gi . . . Phil, I think Spelling's going to try to kill him at the Academy Awards dinner tomorrow night. Listen, if you read those notes carefully, you . . ."

"Can't," Phil said impatiently, and I knew that if he was here standing next to me I'd either shut up now or find out what it felt like to be thrown down Mrs. Plaut's always clean and carpeted stairs.

"Why?"

"There's a war on," he said. "The Japs are getting suicidal. The R.A.F. is bombing Berlin."

"So?"

"So Mick Veblin is district supervisor," Phil said. "You know Mick Veblin?"

"No," I said.

"G. Lane Price, the chief of police of Glendale, knows him. Very well. I'm under investigation for not arresting you when there was sufficient evidence. And Mick is also curious about how I let Wally Hospodar get shot in the back seat of an unmarked police vehicle and why said vehicle is a mess. I have very little credibility here, Toby, and I'll be lucky to hold onto my job."

"I'm sorry, Phil."

"Hell," he said. "Let's just call it a birthday present from you to me."

"Birth—? Phil. It's your birthday."

"Every year at this time."

"I forgot."

"You always do," he said. "But I really don't give a shit.

You're on your own with Varney, and Veblin himself will probably want to talk to you."

"What do you want me to say to him?"

"What do I . . . Toby, I want you to lie your ass off and save my job. Can you do that?"

"I can do that."

"Fine."

"Listen, Phil . . ."

He hung up hard.

So the Los Angeles Police Department was out. It was going to be up to the second team. If I was lucky, I could reach Hy at Hy's for Him on Melrose before he closed. Gunther had his own tux, but Hy, who catered to the lost, lonely, and the once famous, had a tux in the back room that fit me, plus one for a giant and another for a small fat man who sweated a lot.

I was feeling less sorry for myself already.

Chapter 12

I called Hy. I had done some odd jobs for him over the years—tracking his missing mother-in-law, spending a night looking through a hole in the dressing-room wall to catch an employee who was making off with the merchandise, persuading a couple of down-and-outers to make a final and complete payment for goods. I wouldn't say Hy owed me, but then again being nice to people you do business with is good business. Hy was in and was willing to give me a rate on the tuxedos. I didn't tell him money was no object.

I got in my Crosley and headed for Hy's, listening to "A Date with Judy" on the radio. "Night and day, at home or away, always carry Tums," the announcer said. I thought it was a good idea. For the next fifteen minutes, Judy Foster displayed acute anxiety to her brother Randolph about whether Oogie Pringle would call her about the most important school dance of the year.

I double-parked on Melrose right in front of Hy's shop, under the red-on-white banner reading, "Absolutely Everything Must Go Even If It Breaks Me." A cartoon of Hy, complete with sad bulldog face and suspenders over a little belly, looked down at those of us seeking a bargain at his expense.

Hy was at the door with the three boxes. I took them.

"How's business?" I asked.

"Between you and me," he said, looking around the busy shop to be sure no one was listening, "not so bad. Saturdays people buy like there's no tomorrow. I tell them there's no tomorrow. The newspapers tell them there might not be a tomorrow. And me, I lost my lease and everything must go."

"You own the building, Hymie," I reminded him.

"I am not always easy on myself. You got a formal occasion or are you gonna dress up like a waiter again?"

"Academy Awards dinner," I said.

"Ooh, Coconut Grove. The whole schmeer. Best actor's gonna be Gary Cooper. *Pride of the Yankees*. Two years in a row. First Alvin York. Then Lou Gehrig. Can't beat the combo. You can bet on it. My sister's husband delivers sandwiches to the Academy. He heard. Bet on it."

Hy had his thumbs in his suspenders and was rocking from his toes to his heels, Judge Priest himself.

"Can I use your phone?"

"You can use my sister if you promise to marry her."

"You've got a sister?"

"Three of them. All unmarried. Youngest is forty-one, give or take a couple years. Seriously, you want to meet them? Their offspring will be heirs to this gold mine and a couple of outlet stores in Pismo and Venice."

"I want a phone, Hy."

"A phone you got. Think about the sisters though. I'm serious."

Boxes in hand, I moved around Hy and down the aisles, past couples haggling with middle-aged and ancient salesmen and women.

"I call it a miracle," a sunken-chested old salesman with a pencil-thin mustache and badly dyed hair was saying to a young man in front of a shop mirror.

The young man had a short military haircut and darting

eyes that gave him away as someone who was about to ship out.

"Fits like . . . I don't know what," the salesman said, stepping back to admire the young man, who was trying on a tweed jacket with leather elbow patches. A good twenty years too old for the kid. But then again, who knew if the kid had twenty more years.

The salesman—it was Jack-Jack Benoit, who used to deal blackjack in Reno—grabbed my arm. I almost dropped my boxes.

"Stranger," he said. "Does that or does that jacket not fit this young man like perfection? And the colors, textures. I'd swear it was custom-made in England for you."

"Looks great," I said.

The kid wasn't so sure. Jack-Jack needed more help from me, and I knew he was supporting a lot of people on his commission. But I had no heart for even a small con. I plodded onward, the voice of Jack-Jack Benoit behind me saying, "Did I tell you or did I tell you?" to the kid in the tweed jacket. "Now we get this fitted and let's look at some real bargains, vat-dyed twill shirts for two dollars and ninety-four cents, five pair of army socks for one buck."

The place was busy, but no one else stopped me for fashion advice. I pushed into Hy's office, plunked the boxes on the floor, and sat at Hy's desk, a small jungle of pins, needles, thread, and pieces of cloth. I started calling. Everyone should be home by now if home was where they were going.

I tried Shelly at the office. No answer. I tried Shelly at home. Mildred.

"Mildred, my love," I said. "Is your husband home?"

"What does she look like?" Mildred asked.

"Who?"

"The receptionist you hired, the one you insisted that Sheldon help pay for. You know who."

"Violet?"

"Her name is Violet?"

"My business is booming," I said. "I can't keep up with the paperwork, billing, correspondence. Mrs. Gonsenelli is experienced and I've known her family since . . . well, she's like a daughter to me. Mildred, don't tell me you're jealous. Not Mildred Minck."

"Sheldon doesn't need a receptionist," she said. "Sheldon needs a leash. He's run through most of our money with bad investment advice from you and I don't want him to start spending money on some kid who winks at him and pats his bald head. I'm holding you responsible."

Hy opened the door, started to come in, saw I was on the phone, and backed out.

"Reluctantly and with a full understanding of the enormity of the situation, I accept full responsibility. Now can I talk to Sheldon or do I have to have Brink's deliver a quart of my blood to your door as a sign of good faith?"

Mildred hung up. I called back. Shelly answered.

"Toby, you're going to have to apologize to Mildred."

"If it's that or sign on with the Japs as a kamikaze pilot, I'll pack my bags for the Orient."

"Good, I'll tell her you apologize and that you're going to send her flowers."

"You're wasting your money, Shel. Listen, good news. I've got your tux and we're going to the Academy Awards tomorrow night. We're going to keep an eye on Lionel Varney."

"Lionel Varney?"

"The actor who . . . I'll drop your tux off at the office. You come for it in the morning."

"The Academy Awards dinner, you said."

"Rubbing elbows with Kate Hepburn and Ronald Colman," I assured him.

There was a scraping of objects and the vacuum sound of Sheldon putting his hand over the phone.

"Shel?"

He came back on with, "Mildred wants to go."

"No."

"Then I'm not going," he said.

"You mean that?"

"No," he said emphatically. "Besides, Mildred was planning to visit her brother Al in San Diego tomorrow and I have to clean the office."

"You'll pick up the tux in the morning and meet me in front of the Farraday at five?"

"Yes," he said. "That I will do."

He hung up. I got through to Jeremy after two rings.

"The best laid plans have run for the border," I said. Then I told him what had happened. He agreed to join Shelly and me.

"Did you absorb anything that I told you this afternoon about doing things like this?" Jeremy asked.

"Last time," I said. "Promise. The man needs our help. The police won't . . ."

"The conceptual impossibility and magic of infinity is that the human mind is incapable of imagining that beyond the final barrier of space there is something which can be called nothing."

"That a fact?" I said as Hy returned, gave me a two-shouldered shrug, and pointed to his watch.

"You are incapable of conceiving nothingness, Toby. If I am present, you will ask and I will answer. I will be in front of the Farraday in the tuxedo at five tomorrow."

"Thank you, Jeremy," I said. "One more thing. Is there a phone in that model apartment you gave me the key for and do you know the number?"

There was a phone and he knew the number. I thanked him, hung up, and called Gable's house in Encino.

Gable answered on the twelfth ring just as I was about to give up. I told him about Varney, the tuxedos, the police, and the plan.

"And you want me to get you into the Academy Awards dinner?" he asked when I was done.

"You've got it," I said.

Long pause at the other end and then, "Give me numbers where I can reach you. Half hour, maybe an hour from now."

I gave him my office, home number, and the number in Jeremy's model apartment. Hy was standing there patiently above me.

"Want to say hello to Clark Gable?" I asked.

"You kiddin'? I've sold dresses to Spring Byington and three suits in twenty minutes to John Garfield. Star struck I am not. He wants a good discount, he can stop by and I'll see what I'll see."

"Good-bye," I told Gable and hung up.

When I got back out on the street in front of Hy's a uniformed policewoman was just plunking a ticket under my windshield wiper for double-parking.

"I was picking up tuxedos for the Academy Awards dinner," I explained.

She was not young and she was not impressed. "Writer? Actor? What?" she asked, holding the car door open for me.

"Security," I said, working my packages over the seat into the back of the Crosley. No mean task.

"Then you should know better than to double-park," she said.

"Excitement," I said.

She removed the ticket from under the windshield wiper, handed it to me, and said, "Reminder."

I closed the door and drove to Jeremy's model apartment

after stopping at the Farraday and leaving the tuxes. When I got to the apartment and opened the door to the smell of freshly sawed wood and new carpet, I searched for the phone and found it in the kitchen. I wasn't going back to Mrs. Plaut's, not till I knew for sure what Spelling had in mind for me, Varney, Gable, and who knows who else.

Two more calls, one to Gunther, who said his tux was pressed and ready. Another to Varney, who still wasn't back in his room. I figured he was reasonably safe, at least if Jeremy was right and Spelling's clues did mean that he would go for Varney at the Oscar dinner.

It was after six by now, at least that's what I guessed. My father's watch said it was two.

I went out to a neighborhood diner for a pair of BLTs and a couple of Pepsis and talked to the waitress about her nephews in the army and the sorry state of her legs. Armed with a full stomach, the remainder of Clark Gable's advance, and the prospect of a hell of a time the next night, I got back in the Crosley, made a stop, and then drove to Anne's apartment building and rang the bell.

Anne and I had been married for five years. We'd been divorced for seven years. She had remarried Howard, an airline executive who met a death which some people thought was not untimely.

Nothing. I rang again. Beyond the glass door I could hear footsteps coming down the stairs and then I saw Anne peek around the dark-wood banister at me. She took another step and stood on the landing behind the door, about five steps up, hands on her ample hips.

I grinned and gestured at the locked knob. She didn't grin back. I pulled the bouquet of mixed flowers from behind my back and held it up to the door.

"Annie, Annie was the miller's daughter," I sang softly in a not-bad baritone. "Far she wandered from the singing water.

Idle, idle Annie went a-maying. Up hill down hill went her flock a straying. Hear them. Hear them calling as they roam. Annie, Annie bring your white black sheep home."

She mouthed something. I think it was "shit," though Anne was always a lady. Then she came down and opened the door. I held out the flowers. She took them.

"Toby," she said. "We had an agreement. You call if you have to see me."

"And you say no," I reminded her.

"My right," she said.

"It's Phil's birthday," I said.

"So?"

"Can I come in?"

"I've got company," she said, blocking the way, posies in the port-arms position.

"I don't think so," I said.

"What makes you think I'm lying?"

"You're not dressed for company. You're dressed for a night in the bathtub, reading a book, listening to the radio, thinking about old times. Five minutes."

"It's never five minutes, Toby," she said, still barring the entrance.

She was wearing makeup but not much, just what she must have had on during the day. Her hair was dark and billowy and soft, but combed for comfort, not to impress. Her blue blouse was clean but not new and she was wearing slacks.

"We talk here," she said. "We talk fast."

"You look great," I said. "You smell great. I miss you. How about dinner, breakfast, lunch, a hot dog, an ice cream, a walk on the beach, a movie? That cover everything fast enough?"

"Stop, Toby," she said.

"Did I say you smell great?"

"Yes."

"Looks like we're out of conversation."

"Looks like," she said, folding her arms, the flowers dangling. "Toby, please. I've got a new job, long hours, and I'm going to night school."

"School?"

"Law school," she said. "Ridgely Law in the valley."

"Ridgely Law?"

"I'm a little older than the others but I'm told veterans will be coming back and . . ."

"How did you? . . ."

"Marty Lieb knows some people, the dean," Anne said, shifting her eyes past me to the street behind my back.

"Marty? My lawyer?"

"I've gone to him for advice since Howard died and he's been . . ."

"You've been seeing Marty Lieb?" I asked.

Anne didn't answer.

"I need to make it on my own," she said. "And I don't need to go back to reminders of you or Howard. Now, I've got to go."

"Is Marty up there?" I said, pointing to the stairway.

"I told you I have company," she said. "What am I doing here? What am I hiding and apologizing for? Go, Toby. Say happy birthday to Phil for me. Take your flowers back."

She held up her hand with a pushing motion to show that she wanted to close the door.

"I still love you, Anne," I said.

"That was never the problem, Toby. The problem was and is that you are a klutzy Peter Pan, an adult who won't grow up. A . . . oh, what is the use. We've been through this at least four hundred times. I've wasted too many days and nights in the forest about this. Good night."

"Ice cream at Ferny's," I tried as she pushed the door and I backed away. "What can it hurt?"

"I'm too fat now," she said.

"You are voluptuous," I said, holding out the flowers as she continued to ease me through the door.

Before the door slammed shut, she took the flowers.

"I'll call you," I said as the door clicked shut.

She stood there for an instant, eyes moist, or was that my imagination? Then she shook her head, turned, and hurried up the stairs and around the bend.

"Marty Lieb," I said aloud.

If I were a drinking man, I'd have gone out for a couple. If I had the heart for it, I would have called Carmen the cashier for a last-minute date for an Abbott and Costello and a late dinner, even if it meant bringing her son. Instead, I found a shop on Ventura where they sold radios and phonographs and albums. It was almost ten when I got to Ruth and Phil's house in North Hollywood. Ruth answered the door, gave me a hug, and touched my cheek. I was always careful when I hugged my sister-in-law, even before she had gotten sick. There wasn't much of her but heart.

"Kids are asleep," she said. "Phil's not home. Still at work. Some kind of problem."

"You feeling all right, Ruth?"

"Not bad," she said.

And she was right. More pale than usual. Thinner than I remembered. Three kids to take care of and my brother Phil for a husband.

"Come in for a coffee," she said.

She was wearing a robe and was definitely ready for bed and needing it.

"No," I said, handing her the package I was carrying, an Arvin portable in leatherette for Phil's office, if he still had one after the investigation.

"He'll be sorry he missed you," Ruth said, taking the package.

"I'll give you a call tomorrow," I said, taking a step back.

"Maybe we can all go out to Levy's for dinner Monday or Tuesday. On me. Good night, Ruth."

The phone was ringing when I returned to Jeremy's model apartment. It was Clark Gable with the news that Jeremy, Shelly, Gunther, and I were to meet Mame Stoltz in front of the Coconut Grove at six-thirty.

"You'll be there?" I asked.

"I will not be there," Gable said. "But I won't leave town till you let me know what happens."

He wished us luck and I hung up, brushed my teeth with the spare toothbrush I carried in my glove compartment, and shaved with a Gillette razor I'd picked up on the way back.

And then I went to sleep. It had been a long day.

Chapter 13

Saturday, March 4, 1943, was the fifteenth and last time the Academy Awards were given at a more or less intimate banquet for about 200 people. It was also the last and only time someone was murdered at an Oscar-night celebration. The next year, the Academy would move to Grauman's Chinese Theater on Hollywood Boulevard. More than two thousand people would fill the theater. The next year, not only the best actor and actress would receive Oscars, but so would the best supporting actor and actress, who still had to be content with plaques this year.

Next year it wouldn't be an insiders' event anymore, but in 1943 it was still the way it used to be.

I woke up late, wondering what time it was, and realized I had a backache from sleeping in a bed instead of on the floor. I rolled off the side of the bed, sat up, considered cursing the massive Negro gentleman who had given me the bear hug that sent me sleeping on floors. The man who had given me the bear hug was a Mickey Rooney fan. My job had been to keep fans away from Mick at a premiere. I succeeded. It cost me a healthy back and I was paid twenty bucks for the night.

I crawled to the bathroom, wiggled out of my shorts, turned on the shower, hot and hard, and climbed up the wall.

I didn't feel much like singing the score of *No, No Nanette*, but I did manage a medley of "It Seems to Me I Heard That Song Before" and "Always in My Heart."

There are four things I can do when my back goes out. Any one of them has a fifty-fifty chance of helping. I can take a handful of pills Shelly supplied me with about a year ago. But that makes me sleep. I can have Jeremy put his knee in my back. But that hurts. I can sit on the floor, close my eyes, and visualize my pain floating away. Gunther's contribution. But that takes too long. Or I can go see Doc Hodgdon, the orthopedic surgeon who beat me almost every time we played handball at the Y on Hope Street. Doc is pushing seventy and he favors heat, massage, concentration, and pain pills. But Doc Hodgdon was visiting one of his sons back east.

One of the great and terrible things about living alone is that you can groan as much as you want in the shower without worrying about who it might worry. I tried to let that thought carry me past a sudden wave of Anne-itis, a wave that included a glimpse of Attorney Martin Lieb, who deserved to be disbarred for alienation of something.

After ten minutes, I turned off the shower and found that I could walk, not the way I had the night before, but movement was possible. I was struggling into my shorts when the doorbell rang. I considered ignoring it. It rang. And it kept ringing. I ached my way back to the bedroom, forced my legs into my wrinkled pants, and headed for the door, which was four or five miles away.

The doorbell stopped ringing, but I kept moving.

To the extent that I figured at all, I figured that it was Jeremy coming to show the apartment but unable to get in because I had the key. Or it was a would-be renter. Or it was a plumber, painter, steam fitter, carpet cleaner, carpenter, or lost woodpecker. I opened the door. Spelling was standing there in a blue mechanic's uniform carrying a large gun in his right hand.

"I'm not dressed yet," I said. "If you can come back in about ten minutes . . ."

Spelling looked over his shoulder into the courtyard. There was no one in sight. He motioned me back with his gun and I stepped back as he came in and kicked the door shut.

"How long have you been at this?" he asked.

"This?"

"The detective business," he said. "Twenty years? More? And you can't tell when someone is following you? You're in the wrong career."

"A little late for me to change," I said. "Mind if I put my shirt on."

"Go ahead," he said, looking around the room.

I put on my shirt and considered my options. There weren't many. My back was bad. My gun was in the glove compartment of the Crosley. I had to resort to persuasion.

"Have you figured anything out yet?" he asked, sitting on the edge of the bed. "My clues weren't very subtle."

"We've got some ideas," I said.

"You picked up three tuxedos at some place called Hy's for Him. And you went to see a lady who didn't want to see you. I'll give you one thing. You didn't look sorry for yourself."

My shirt was a little fragrant from a day of wear and a night draped over a chair, but I didn't think it mattered.

"It gets worse," I said. "My back went out this morning."

"Lower, upper?" Spelling asked.

"Lower."

"Turn around. I know a way to end your pain."

"I can live with it," I said.

"Turn," he ordered.

I turned.

"Take it easy," he said softly. "Easy."

I felt the steel of the gun against my shoulder and two hands digging into my shoulders. Then something drove into my lower back and I thought I'd been done in by a silencer. I doubled forward on the floor, feeling sick to my stomach.

"Don't go into a ball," Spelling ordered. "Stay loose.

"I'm loose," I groaned. "I'm loose."

"You and your friends are going formal tonight, right? Any place I might know?"

"No," I said. "Birthday. My brother's."

"In soup and fish?"

"His fiftieth," I said. "Big cele . . ."

"Shut up."

I shut up and rolled to a semisitting position with my elbows on the floor.

"You can't stop me, Peters," he said, pointing the gun at my face. "They killed my father and then they went on with their lives, just did what they wanted. Until I showed up and killed them."

"Not all of them," I said.

"Not yet," he said. "Stand up."

I stood, using the bed for support.

"Now twist around on your waist. Don't turn the shoulders."

I did it.

"How's it feel?" he asked.

"Not bad," I said.

"Good," said Spelling. "I want you alive and well when I kill you."

"I appreciate that," I said.

"I'm going now," he said. "I just wanted you to know that you can't hide from me. And I wanted you . . ."

"Hold it," I said, reasonably sure that Spelling was not going to kill me now. "How much longer is this going to go on? You fixed my back, maybe. But you are one pompous son of a bastard, and gratitude will only go so far. So, hostage crisis or not, either shoot me or get the hell out of here."

"You're pretty goddamn impatient to die, Peters. I'm going to leave," he said, backing through the bedroom to the front door.

I took a step toward him, half expecting him to begin firing. But he didn't. When he cleared the door I hurried to the window. My back was pretty good, not a hundred percent, but good. I could get my .38 from the glove compartment and run after him, but I knew I couldn't run and I knew I couldn't shoot straight at more than ten feet. The time to use a gun is when you're sure the other guy doesn't have one.

I found my shoes and socks and put them on with new problems to think about. Why had Spelling come here? Why did he want me to figure out his poetic clues? And, most important, why the hell hadn't he shot me?

I needed a bowl of Wheaties fast.

I had a day to kill or be killed in. I went back to Phil's house. This time he was home. He opened the door, not happy to see me, and stepped back so I could enter. He looked awful. Red eyes, scrub forest of hair on his face. Walking around in his stocking feet.

I went in and I followed him through the small living room complete with photographs of his family on the fake fireplace, and matching sofa and chairs worn thin from jumping kids.

"Coffee?" he asked, sitting down at the kitchen table.

I nodded. Phil poured. Ruth was a good cook. Brisket. Pot roast. Turkey. Kreplach. Matzo-ball soup. Spaghetti and mean meatballs, but there was no heart in her coffee. But Phil was a quantity man; he was content if there was plenty of Maxwell House and it was hot and black.

We drank.

"Got any Wheaties?" I asked.

Phil didn't answer. He simply rose, went to a cabinet, produced an orange Wheaties box, and went for a couple of bowls and the milk bottle.

We drank and ate for a while without talking. Then, "Spelling followed me to an apartment I was staying in," I said. "Came to the door with a gun."

"That a fact?" said Phil, without bothering to look at me.

"A fact. Don't you want to know why I'm not dead?"

"Why aren't you dead?" Phil asked indifferently, and took a sip of coffee.

"I don't know," I said. "I think he wants me at the Academy Awards dinner tonight. I think he plans to kill Varney in front of the stars and cameras. I think he wants the newspapers, *Look*, *Life*, and N.B.C. to cover it so he can tell the world how his father was destroyed by Hollywood."

Phil was eating his Wheaties and shaking his head no.

"What do you mean, *no?* He could walk in there tonight with a Thompson and mow down Bob Hope, Rosalind Russell, Ronald Colman, Irving Berlin, and . . . and Turhan Bey."

"No," Phil said, finishing his Wheaties and working on the dregs with a tilted bowl. "At least, not because his father was done in by heartless Hollywood." Phil put down his bowl. "We, the police department of Los Angeles, did some research. First, the guy who calls himself Spelling is not Spelling. Second, I know this because the Spelling who died with a sword in the middle of his gut on *Gone With the Wind* had no sons, no daughters, no nieces, and no nephews. Orphan. Never married."

"That doesn't make sense," I said, pushing my empty bowl and half-full cup away.

"Doesn't have to make sense, Tobias," Phil said. "It's true, but it doesn't have to make sense."

"So why is he telling everyone he's Spelling's son? Why is he killing these people? Why does he want to kill Varney? And maybe Gable? Why does he write poems and . . ."

"He's a crazy," said Phil. "We catch him. He maybe talks. Maybe doesn't talk. Maybe makes some kind of weird sense. Maybe makes no sense. We've both seen them. They scare the hell out of you. They make me mad. With crazies you've got nothing to count on."

"No," I said. "I don't buy that explanation while there's still a copy of *Casket and Sunnyside* on the shelf."

Phil suddenly brought his hand down on the bowl. It shattered. I looked at his clenched fist. Somehow, his hand wasn't bleeding.

"Phil?"

He looked across at me. "I'm on suspension," he said, on the verge of more explosions. "Maybe pushed into retirement. There wouldn't be a *maybe* about it if the war was over and the place was running with M.P.'s looking for work. You know what my record looks like, Toby?"

"You've worked the streets and you're honest," I said.

"I break heads and I've got a bad temper."

"You?"

Phil scratched the back of his closed right fist. A very, very bad sign.

"I think I'll be going now, Phil," I said, getting up.

He looked at me but didn't answer, and I got up.

"Tell Ruth and the kids I stopped by. Happy birthday."

"Monday, Veblin's office, Toby. You lie. You save my job. I've got nothing but that job."

He advanced on me and we were face to face, inches apart. Déjà vu, a thousand times like this, maybe two thousand since I was four.

"I'm not putting on a security uniform and punching a warehouse time clock," he said.

"I'll lie," I promised.

"Good night, Toby."

"Good night, Phil."

I left.

There had been much better days and this one could have been worse. It couldn't have been much more confusing but it could have been worse, at least for me. I was still alive.

My things were in the Crosley. I wondered if Spelling had followed me to Phil's. I looked around. Nothing, but then again I hadn't spotted him before. But then again, I hadn't been looking before.

No point in going back to Jeremy's model apartment. I headed for Mrs. Plaut's and made it there in about an hour. There was no waiting landlady. The house was quiet. I took off my shoes and tiptoed up the stairs slowly. In my room, I turned on the lights and put my bag on the sofa.

Dash sat on the table. He didn't purr. He didn't scold or make noise. He waited for food. I gave him some and then I kicked off my pants and threw my shirt on the chair. I was too tired to wash, too tired to shave, too tired to think, and my back was starting to complain again. I turned off the lights, plopped on my mattress, and hugged my third pillow.

My fingers touched something, paper. I groaned and sat up, crawling to the light with the paper in my hand. I found the switch and looked at the envelope, a Selznick International envelope complete with the drawing of the Selznick office building in the corner. My name was on it. I opened it. Single sheet. Simple message.

"Tomorrow has finally come."

I hit the light switch, lay back, and closed my eyes.

When I opened them, I discovered that Spelling or whoever he was was right. Tomorrow had come. The sun was coming through the window and my back hurt. A lesser man or a greater one would have been discouraged. There were three things to do. First, I lifted Dash off of my stomach. His claws tickled my skin and his weight threatened my lower back. Second, I pulled myself up by the couch and balanced, clutching the pink-and-blue pillow Mrs. Plaut had given me, with "God Bless Us Every One" stitched in pink on blue. I staggered slowly to the refrigerator, pulled out the nearly empty bottle of milk and an almost-full box of Hydrox vanilla cookies with the cream centers.

I made it to the table, kicked the chair a few inches from the table, and sat. There was a reasonably clean coffee cup on the table. I filled it with milk and began dunking cookies. After six cookies I was feeling decidedly better, not yet human or able to walk, but with something to live for. After six more cookies, I was confident that life had meaning, but what that meaning might be was nowhere near my understanding.

I was considering whether to finish the last three cookies and the rest of the milk when the door opened.

"Toby," said Gunther, dressed, pressed, and ready for the day in a three-piece suit and perfectly matched striped tie. "What is wrong?"

"Wrong?" I said with a grin. "Nothing. My brother's about to lose his job and it's my fault. My ex-wife, who, by the way, I still love, is seeing my lawyer. My back is out. I am nearly broke and I've got an actor to protect and a killer to catch who makes no sense."

"That, if I may say so, does not seem that unusual for you," said Gunther with concern.

"I'm running out of cookies," I tried.

"That," he said, "can be remedied. It is the look of protective madness in your eyes that concerns me."

"I'll be fine," I assured him.

"You have a phone call," he said.

I nodded wisely and stood up, with effort.

"Some focused meditation would help your back," he said.

I grunted and used the furniture and the walls to make it past Gunther and inch my way along the wall toward the phone.

"I suggest you lean against me," he said.

I grunted again and leaned against Gunther, which made my back hurt even more but I didn't have the heart to turn down his offer of help. Gunther was sensitive about his size.

"Hello," I said.

"You got my note?"

"What's your name?"

"I didn't sign it, but you know my name. Spelling."

"Nope. Try again. Spelling had no relatives," I said.

"Not officially."

"Not unofficially either," I said. "I just read the autopsy report. Lots of stuff I didn't understand, but I did understand this—he couldn't have children. Born that way."

No sound on the other end at my less-than-brilliant but apparently effective lie. I was feeling better already.

"Let's hear a poem," I suggested. "The day is young."

"The actor dies tonight," he said, probably between clenched teeth. "And then you."

"Good-bye," I said and hung up.

I was feeling much, much better, though I didn't know why. Gunther stayed with me while I called Shelly at the office. Violet Gonsenelli answered, all businesslike, "Dr. Minck's office."

"Dr. Minck and Private Investigator Peters," I corrected.

"Dr. Minck told me . . ."

"Minck and Peters, like The Spirit and Ebony, Plastic Man and Woozy Winks, Captain Midnight and Ichabod Mudd," I said.

"I don't understand," Violet said.

"Is this the first call you've taken?"

"Yes."

"It gets more confusing," I said. "Let me talk to Shelly."

I talked to Shelly, fast, few words, and to the point. And then I turned to find myself facing the new boarder.

Her sudden appearance didn't dampen my senseless glee. I couldn't remember her name, but I'll never forget the look she gave me as Gunther and I said good morning and she hurried down the stairs.

"I don't think she cares for you, Gunther," I said.

"I suggest it is your countenance which disturbed her, Toby," he said.

I was dressed only in a pair of undershorts of doubtful cleanliness and protection. I needed a shave, a shower, a comb, and the impression that I could stand without the support of a wall and a very little person.

"What's your day like, Gunther?" I asked.

"Well, it is in fact a rather complex one, Toby," he said, helping me back to my room and to the chair at the table. "I have a luncheon engagement with Miss Stoltz, and Gwen is in the city and has asked if I could possibly meet with her at some point. I was thinking of tea or, perhaps . . . did you need my services before tonight?"

"No," I said. "Just so you're in your tux and ready by six."

"I will be," Gunther said. "If you have need of my help before eleven twenty-two, simply knock on the wall. I will be working."

And Gunther departed.

Ten minutes later I made my way to the bathroom down the hall, carrying a pair of pants and a shirt from the closet. My pants from the night before were still on the floor. I could think of no way of picking them up and then coming to anything like a standing position without massive military assistance.

I managed to shower, shave, shampoo, clean my ears with Q-tips, brush my teeth, and look myself in the face in the mirror.

I wasn't perfect, but I was better and better. I sat on the

sofa, clutched Mrs. Plaut's pillow, looked down at Dash who was washing himself, and fell asleep.

Koko the Clown came in the room. He had a big orange drum with the words "University of Illinois" printed on it in blue letters. He was banging the drum and singing, "Cincinnati, Cincinnati," over and over again in a voice I recognized but couldn't place.

"No," I muttered.

"Yes," said Koko, banging the drum so hard that it split. Little penguins began to leap out of the drum. They looked around the room, looked at me, and went for the refrigerator. One stood on another and then another and another till they could reach the handle. I tried to say no again but I couldn't move and Koko was banging on my stomach.

He was whispering something. I hoped it wasn't Cincinnati.

"When are the unborn born? When are the dead not dead?" he said. It was Spelling's voice.

"How the hell should I know?" I said, or thought I said. "Riddle me no damn riddles and get those damn penquins back in the drum and away from my last three Hydrox cookies."

Koko was a foot tall and standing on the floor looking up at me with hands on his hips. The little white ball of yarn on the peak of his pointed cap was rippling from a sourceless wind.

"Penguin," he said.

"That's what I said."

"You said *penquin*," Koko corrected. "How can you catch me if you don't catch the little mistakes."

The penguins turned. I don't know how many of them. Each one had a Hydrox cookie in its beak. They were moving toward me and growing bigger. I tried to back away, scream, but I couldn't. Then I opened my eyes.

Shelly, Jeremy, and Gunther stood before me wearing tuxedos. Shelly's neck was pinched and his face was red. He held out his hand, palm-up, and handed me three white pills. I took them and put them in my mouth. He handed me a glass of water. I drank it and handed the glass back.

"No penquins in Cincinnati," I said.

Jeremy lifted me under the arms and turned me around. I was still clutching Mrs. Plaut's pillow and I was facing the wall. Jeremy said something and then I felt a sudden whaap just above my rear end. Jeremy sat me down again and I handed him the pillow. He gave it to Gunther.

"Sit quietly a minute or two," Jeremy said.

I blinked and sat quietly. Shelly handed me the glass of water again. I finished it. It was warm.

"I'm okay now," I said.

"See if you can stand," Jeremy said.

I was slow, careful, but I could stand and the pain was gone. I'd had results like this before from Shelly's pills and Jeremy's knee and arms. It might last for days or weeks. Then again, my back might be worse than before in a few hours.

"Time?" I asked, trying to focus on the Beech-Nut clock.

"A few minutes after six," Gunther said, looking at his big pocket watch.

"Got to get into my tux," I said.

"We put it on you," Shelly said, trying to breathe.

I looked down.

"How do I look?"

"Functional," said Jeremy.

"Then," I said, blowing out the bad air and brushing my hair back with my palms. "Let's go to a party."

Chapter 14

Mame Stoltz was waiting for us in front of the Ambassador Hotel where the Academy and its guests were arriving. She was wearing a black lacy gown with pearls around her neck. When she saw us, she dropped the cigarette she had been working on, ground it out with the sole of her black high-heeled pump, and said, "You're late."

"Parking was difficult and Toby has been a bit beneath the weather," said Gunther, taking her hand. "You look lovely."

I give it to Mame. She didn't look around to see how the gathering crowd was reacting to the tender moment between the little man and the not-little woman.

"Gunther's right. You look awful, Toby," she said.

"You should have seen him twenty minutes ago," said Shelly, looking around for celebrities.

Mame led us past a Movietone crew interviewing Bing Crosby, who gave nods and waves to the fans gathering, calling, cheering. Photographers were taking pictures of everyone, including us.

Lieutenant Van Heflin, wearing his dress army uniform, walked in ahead of us with a dark serious woman on his arm.

"I tell you that's Billy Barty," a woman said.

"The other one," someone squealed. "That's Sydney Green-street. I didn't know he wore such thick glasses."

"That one. That one," came another female voice. "I'll bet that's Van Heflin's father."

I turned as we kept moving. The woman was pointing at me. Mame nodded and the two uniformed doormen backed by two uniformed security guards parted and we marched in. Shelly picked up the rear. He was grinning and waving to the crowd, who waved back.

"I could have been an actor," Shelly said as we followed Mame through the crowded lobby.

Many of the men were in uniform. In fact, the Academy had claimed that 27,677 members of the industry were in the military. A fact that accounted for Lionel Varney's triumphant return to Hollywood. I was looking for Lionel as we walked. I saw Tyrone Power in his marine private's dress uniform talking to Alan Ladd in his air-corps private's uniform. Power was about my height. Ladd barely reached his shoulders, but his eyes met mine and I was the one who turned away.

A young woman in a maid's uniform came past us with a tray of what looked like whipped eggs on Ritz crackers. Shelly grabbed three of them, almost knocking the woman over.

"Through here," Mame said over her shoulder.

"Why's the skinny guy here?" Shelly asked, nodding at a man in a corner talking to a tall, thin blonde with the reddest lips and whitest teeth I'd ever seen.

"That's Irving Berlin," Mame said. "Stop gawking and get in here."

Mame closed the door when we had all piled into a room with a white wooden conference table surrounded by white matching chairs with gold trim. The table was clean and clear except for four pairs of white gloves.

"Gable said to tell you that he was going to Georgia for a

little while but then he'd be heading home to wait for your report on what happens."

"Right," I said.

"Through that door is the kitchen," Mame said, fishing a
fresh cigarette from a pack in her purse.

Gunther reached up to light it for her with a match which
had magically appeared in his small hand.

"Beyond the kitchen is the Coconut Grove," she said. "The
Universal table is to the left of the door beyond the kitchen.
Three tables over. When the program starts, you can go into
the Grove. Miguel, the assistant head waiter, will give you
something to carry and tell you where to put it down. Then
you just stand against a wall with your hands folded in front
of you trying to look above the whole damn thing. Here."

She handed each of us a pair of the white gloves. Mine fit
fine, which made me think that Shelly's and Jeremy's would
be too tight and Gunther's would be too large. Wrong. Everyone had the right-size gloves. Mame had been in the business
for more than two decades. She could gauge a glove size with
a glance.

"Backstage," I said. "One of us has to go backstage. Our
friend Spelling, or whoever he is, may want to put on a little
show. You know, jump out on the stage, shove Bob Hope
aside, and take a few shots at Varney or Maureen O'Hara."

"There isn't much of a backstage area," said Mame. "Presen-
ters come up from their tables and the receivers do the same,
but . . ." She shrugged, taking a deep drag. "If that's what it
takes. Who goes backstage?"

There was only one reasonable choice. I didn't look at him
but Gunther and Shelly did. Jeremy nodded.

"Okay," said Mame. "Come with me."

Mame patted Gunther's cheek and they smiled at each
other. Then she went back into the lobby with Jeremy behind
her.

"I look nothing like Billy Barty," Gunther said with a sigh when they were gone. "Nothing? Am I correct?"

"Nothing," I said.

"You're both short," said Shelly, stuffing the last of the whipped-egg canapés in his mouth. A spot of yellow stuck to his nose.

"Yes, of course," Gunther said with uncharacteristic sarcasm. "How could I have failed to notice that?"

"It's better than being Van Heflin's father," I said.

"I have never seen Van Heflin's father," said Gunther.

We went on like this for about five minutes till Mame returned. "Hurry," she said and pushed open the door that led to the Coconut Grove kitchen.

The kitchen was full of cooks, waitresses, and busboys, bustling busily as quietly as they could. Beyond the door across the room a woman was singing "The Star Spangled Banner."

"Lena Horne," Shelly said, as Mame clicked through the kitchen giving whispered greetings to the staff, who all seemed to recognize her.

There was a small window in the door to the Grove dining room. Mame looked through it, checked her watch, and stepped away, pointing to the left of the window. I moved to the window. A small band was playing and Jeanette MacDonald was standing on a low platform at the far end of the room singing, her mouth wide and trembling. I looked to the left. It took me a few seconds to find Lionel Varney standing next to Turhan Bey. Lionel looked great in the tux. Bey looked even better.

The people in uniform were saluting. The men and women out of uniform had their hands to their hearts.

I looked around for someone who might be Spelling, but it was tough to see much till they all sat down. I did see Jimmy Cagney biting his lower lip and smiling, his eyes fixed on

MacDonald. He'd failed as best actor a few years ago in *Angels with Dirty Faces*. *Variety* and the *Hollywood Reporter* had him neck and neck this year with Ronald Colman. *Yankee Doodle Dandy* was the sentimental favorite, but the Academy was usually in M-G-M's pocket, and *Random Harvest* looked good for Colman.

"Lemme see," said Shelly, putting his face next to mine and nudging me away.

Gunther, who was about three feet short of the window, with no dignified way to look through, stood looking at the kitchen crew scurrying around.

"She's . . ." Shelly said. "Can you believe she's so skinny? I mean she looks like a piece of spaghetti next to Nelson Eddy, but in real life she's worse."

When the anthem was almost done, a dark man in a tux and gloves like ours pushed a silver cart next to us. The man had a receding hairline and a full mustache. Mame introduced him as Miguel and then she clicked away back through the kitchen.

"Pitchers of water," Miguel said. "One for table five." He pointed at me. "One for seven." He pointed at Shelly. "And one for table twelve." He pointed at Gunther. "Directly to the left of the nearest gentleman to the kitchen at each table. Space has been set aside."

"Then," he continued. "You find a place against the wall near the exit to the left," the accented man said to Gunther. "And you stay against the wall and out of the way. If one of the guests should ask you for anything, nod, get the attention of a real waiter by raising your right hand no higher than your shoulder. A waiter will come and you will tell him quietly without bending your head to him what the guest wishes. Understood?"

"Understood," I agreed.

"Good," said the man, looking through the window. "Other

pitchers of water are now being placed on the tables. It is time."

"I'm a dentist," Shelly said to the man.

"We have had physicians, lawyers, and even a senator offer hundred-dollar bills to let them wait tables on Oscar night," the man said.

"State or federal senator?" Shelly said, taking his pitcher.

"From Oregon," the man said, pointing to the door.

Shelly went out, Gunther followed, and I was last. Bob Hope was at the podium making jokes about William Bendix and pretending to be hurt because he wasn't nominated for *The Road to Morocco*. I found my table and put the water pitcher down next to Ronald Reagan. I knew some people sitting at the tables, worked on cases for them. Gary Cooper, Bette Davis, but I didn't figure they'd recognize me or even take a good look. People don't even recognize their own waiter in an uncrowded restaurant after they've given their orders.

I moved to a white wall, careful not to lean on it, and looked around for Gunther and Shelly. Gunther was about twenty yards away to my left. Shelly was the same distance to my right. Shelly had something in his mouth. He adjusted his glasses and gave me a small wave to let me know that we were on the same team and ever alert.

Dinner went fine. Talk, chatter, most of it nervous. Waiters scurrying in and out. Plates clanking. Dessert served. Busboys removing dishes, smoke making the air stale in spite of the air conditioning.

And then the awards.

We stood through *Mrs. Miniver* winning five awards and an acceptance speech by Greer Garson that seemed longer than the movie. Cagney's acceptance speech was short and ended with, "My mother thanks you. My father thanks you. And I thank you."

Much applause. Usually led by Shelly.

Reap the Wild Wind got a Special Effects Oscar, and Irving Berlin gave himself the Oscar for the song "White Christmas," saying, after he opened the envelope, "I'm glad to present the award. I've known the fellow a long time." Not much of a joke, but Hope's jokes didn't get a better round of laughter.

He wasn't coming. I couldn't figure it, but the evening was winding up, with Documentary, Scoring, and Technical and Scientific awards—one went to some guys at Twentieth for the development of a lens-calibration system and the application of this system to exposure control in cinematography.

Varney laughed and clapped in all the right places, listened politely when the stars at his table spoke, and kept his own contribution to a minimum. Two or three times he looked my way and our eyes met. He didn't give anything away.

Now it was just about over and Bob Hope was cracking a few final jokes about the Oscars being made out of plaster this year, because of the war, instead of the usual gold-plated bronze.

It was Shelly who spotted Spelling. Maybe it was because Spelling had spent over an hour in Shelly's dental chair and Shelly had witnessed the sweating pores of the man. Whatever it was, Shelly spotted him.

Spelling had walked past me at least five times in the past few hours with his back to me. And he had gone past me back into the kitchen carrying stacks of plates, piles of ashtrays, and bottles of wine to cover his face.

Shelly was waving wildly. Hope glanced at him, and Dmitri Tiomkin, who was seated near Shelly, actually got up and tried to calm him. I followed Shelly's finger and looked around. Spelling was coming toward me, a water pitcher held at eye level, his face distorted by the water.

I took a step to my right to block the door to the kitchen, and Spelling knew he had been spotted. He put down the water pitcher, shoved his hand into his pocket, and headed for the Universal table and Lionel Varney.

Gunther was the closest. Spelling had three tables and a combination of rising and milling guests and working waiters and busboys to get through. Gunther eased through the crowd, tugged at Varney's sleeve, and pointed at the advancing Spelling. The smile on Varney's face disappeared. He got up and followed Gunther as Spelling began to elbow his way through the crowd. I was after them, but it was tough going. Above the crowd I could see Jeremy also moving through the sea of gowns and tuxedos.

Gunther and Varney went through a door and Spelling hurried after them.

By the time I hit the door, Jeremy was at my side and Shelly was panting behind me. I pushed the door open. A corridor. Restaurant and hotel staff gathering dirty table linen, wheeling those laundry carts that blocked our way.

We grunted through. Gunther, Varney, and Spelling were nowhere in sight. We opened doors on both sides and stuck our heads in those that were closed.

We asked which way the little man had gone. A few people pointed farther down the corridor. At the end of the corridor was an exit sign and a one-way door. We pushed through.

A parking lot filled with big dark cars with teeth, and at the end of the lot not far from the street, an attendant in a white uniform and cap was ducking down behind a Jaguar. I motioned Jeremy and Shelly down and we moved under cover to where the attendant crouched.

"Over there," he said.

Gunther and Varney stood against a brick wall. Spelling stood about a dozen yards in front of them with a gun in his hand. Gunther was talking fast and trying to put himself between Varney and the weapon in Spelling's hand.

There wasn't much light. Just a few low parking-lot bulbs

to lead the way to the waiting cars. The blackout was still in effect. The Japanese might launch an all-out attack from one of their few remaining submarines in the hope of taking out half of Hollywood.

We duck-walked closer, close enough to hear Spelling say, "You're the last, Varney. When you're done, I don't care what happens to me. My father will be revenged."

"Wait," Gunther said. "This is pointless. You cannot get your father back by killing people."

Spelling laughed and said, "A little late for that, little man. Wouldn't make much sense for me to walk away when there's only this one left, this one who has the career my father deserved."

Spelling raised his gun and Jeremy rose and broke into a graceful trot in the direction of the armed man.

"Jeremy, you can't . . ." I called, but he was gone.

Slow motion crept into my stomach. Spelling was already turning to face the sound of the giant running at him.

"Hold it," Spelling called, but Jeremy didn't hold it.

The first shot missed, but I don't think by much. It did tear through the windshield of a Rolls whose window did not shatter. Spelling was lining up for a second shot and Jeremy still had a long way to go.

"This is all wrong," Spelling shouted. "Stop. It's not supposed to be like this. This isn't in the script."

The gun was up. Jeremy was too close and too big a target to miss.

And the shot crackled in the night and echoed across the brick wall behind Gunther and Varney.

I tried to breathe. I tried not to look. But I had to look. Jeremy was still up and running. Spelling had dropped his gun. A splatter of blood stained his shirt. Spelling looked around just before Jeremy barreled into him. He looked at Gunther and Varney and said something I couldn't hear.

Jeremy circled the falling killer with his arms and kept the man from going down. We were all running toward them now. Jeremy laid the dying man on the cement and stood up. Spelling looked around, the odd shadows of the blackout lights setting his eye sockets in a dead darkness. The expression on his face was one of surprise. He reached a hand toward Varney and went limp with a choking gasp.

"He's dead," Shelly said in his best dental-surgery manner.

"What did he say, Jeremy?" I asked.

"He said, 'not in the script.' "

Varney and Gunther came forward slowly. Varney's tie was at a weird angle like a cockeyed propeller. His hair was a tumbled mess and his eyes were wide. I'm not sure if his hands were trembling.

"Who shot him?" Shelly asked.

It seemed a reasonable question. I looked around. The parking-lot attendant had disappeared. From the darkness, between a pair of matching Chryslers, my brother Phil stepped out. He was the only one in the alley not wearing soup and fish. He had on slacks, a tieless white shirt, a zippered Windbreaker, and he was carrying a gun in his right hand.

"I told the kid to call an ambulance," he said, moving closer to the body.

"He's dead," Shelly said.

"Then they can take him to the morgue," Phil said.

It was clear. It was simple. Phil had been convinced that Varney was in danger. He could do nothing officially, so he had backed us up on his own. We stood in a circle looking down at the dead man. I looked up at Phil and we both knew that, barring a miracle, this was probably the end of his career. He had been suspended and had no business in an alley shooting civilians, no matter how much they might deserve it. I looked at Varney, whose eyes were red and confused. He blinked first.

Phil turned his back and started to walk away. I followed him.

"I can still lie," I said.

"Won't be enough," he answered, putting his gun back in the holster under his windbreaker.

Then I had an idea. I turned away.

"Veblin in the morning," I said. "I've got someone to see in Atlanta who might be able to keep you on the streets. Shelly, I need your car keys."

Shelly stood up, reluctantly pulled his keys from his pocket, and threw them to me. "Toby, don't hurt the car," he whined.

I can't say that I ran, but for a man who had been crippled a few hours earlier, I moved reasonably well. I had a plan. None of my friends were dead. Things were starting to make sense.

Shelly's car was jammed between a Ford coupe and a little Chevy. I inched it out and headed for Culver City.

Chapter 15

I used the direct approach and drove right up to the gate at Selznick International. People, some of the men in Confederate and Union uniforms and tuxedos like mine, some of the women in flowing gowns and flashing jewelry, were on their way out. It was light. The night was getting old.

"It's all over," a uniformed guard said, leaning over to my open window and seeing my formal attire. "Sorry, sir."

"I was at the Academy Awards," I explained. "I'll just say a few hellos and . . . no more than ten minutes, promise. I was on security for *Gone With the Wind*. You remember Wally Hospodar? I worked with him."

"Whatever happened to Wally?" the guard asked.

"Dead," I said.

"Heard he hit the skids," said the guard.

"Hard," I said.

"Go on through," he said, waving his hand to the guard a little closer to the gate. "But make it ten minutes. No more."

I drove past the second guard and through the gate that was open just enough for me to make it through. I maneuvered past oncoming cars and a few people walking. I heard a voice, unmistakable, Butterfly McQueen. I kept going and found less traffic as I drove past the hill that looked down at

the burning back-lot Atlanta. No one was there. The charred
wood had long been carted away. Atlanta had been replaced by
what looked like a ranch house in the moonlight.

I drove farther and wended my way to where Tara had
stood. I didn't see any people, but the front of the house was
still there across the field and past the trees. There wasn't anything left of the gate or fence, and the wooden frame of the
house was crumbling, but it was still Tara.

I almost missed him and drove on to see what was left of
the Wilkes house, but a glint of moonlight hit something on
the porch of Tara. I parked and walked across the field, heading for the glow of a cigarette in the darkness.

"Peters," Clark Gable said, stepping down from the porch.
"What the hell are you doing here?"

Gable was in full khaki uniform, including the flight cap.

"Spelling's dead," I said.

He dropped his cigarette in the dirt, stepped on it, sighed
and said, "Then that's that."

"Looks that way," I said.

Gable turned to face Tara.

"I'm shipping back in the morning," he said. "Send the bill
to Encino. Someone will forward it to me."

"I'll do that."

"You look good in a tux," he said with a lopsided grin.

"And you look good in uniform," I said.

He didn't answer for a few seconds and then he said, "I
didn't know how happy I was when we were making that picture. My wife and I were settling down in the house. We were
talking about babies, taking home movies, and planning for
the future. She was a funny woman. A beautiful, funny
woman."

"I need a favor," I said.

"Name it," Gable said, turning to face me.

I told him what I needed and he said, "It'll be done in the morning before I leave. Anything else?"

"One thing," I said. "You know these lines, 'You're the last. When you're done, I don't care what happens to me. My father will be revenged.' "

"Sounds familiar," Gable said. "Let me think. I read it . . . *Gangsters in Concrete*. I was supposed to play a gangster named Marone or Barone, something like that. I think the part went to Clive Brook. Why?"

"Someone played the part badly tonight," I said.

"Wasn't much of a part in the first place," Gable said. "What's this about?"

"About a man dying even though it wasn't in the script," I said.

"Listen, Peters, if you're not going to make sense . . ."

"He's making sense," a voice came from one of Tara's first-floor windows behind Gable.

Gable turned and looked up. I knew what I would see.

Lionel Varney climbed through the window. He had a gun in his hand and he was aiming it down at us.

"Who is this?" Gable said irritatedly. "And what is going on here?"

"You want to tell him, Peters?" asked Varney, who was still in his tux. His tie and hair were straight now, but there was a shake to his hands and his voice that he wasn't a good enough actor to hide.

"You tell him, Spelling," I said.

"Spelling?" asked Gable.

"The way it makes sense is Spelling here killed Lionel Varney the night Atlanta burned over that hill. He had been talking to Varney and found out that he had no relatives. Spelling, here, needed a new identity. He was wanted for outstanding felonies in at least five states."

"I thought you wanted me to tell it," Spelling said. "How

often does an actor get a chance to perform in front of the king himself?"

"Get to the point, whoever you are," Gable said, hands on hips.

"I killed Varney, took his place, and headed back east. I wasn't getting anywhere in Hollywood as Spelling. I thought I might be better off in summer theater as Varney. And then the irony. The damned irony."

He had moved to the edge of the steps now and he was no more than six feet from us, the gun aimed at Clark Gable's face.

"Well," Spelling said with a sigh. "I got this opportunity to return to film, the Universal contract, and I realized that there were a handful of people who might remember me when the publicity started. They might remember me and the fact that they knew me as Spelling, and the man who had died that night as Varney. Normally, they might not remember the face and name of a man met casually, but that had been a special night of burning cities and a soldier who died in a freak accident. So . . . ."

"You came back and started to kill people on the film who might see your picture in the paper or up on the screen and go for the police," Gable said.

"Or blackmail," Spelling answered. "My mistake was hiring Edgar, who I'd met in Quentin about ten years ago."

"Edgar?" Gable asked.

"The one who died tonight," I explained. "The one who said he was Spelling's son. The poems, the clues, the jealousy over lost parts. All a fake to cover the real reason for the murders, to get me to that alley where I'd witness an attempt on your life, a scene taken right out of an old M-G-M programmer. You couldn't even write an original scene. And then it fell apart. 'Not in the script,' Edgar said. My guess is that Edgar was supposed to miss when he took a shot at you and then run away screaming like a loon into the night, never to be heard from again."

"Something like that," Spelling agreed.

"And he was stupid enough to believe you," I said.

"Seems that way, doesn't it," said Spelling.

"Now what?" asked Gable.

"A little tricky," Spelling said. "I'll have to shoot you both, of course. My first thought was that I could make it look like Edgar did it before he appeared in the alley, but that won't work. I guess you'll both have to disappear."

"Like hell I'll disappear," said Gable.

"Not much choice for either of us," Spelling said.

Gable, jaw tight, took a step toward Spelling. Something clicked in the gun. I shouted "Shoot, Phil," and dropped to the ground.

Spelling turned to look for Phil, and Gable leaped up the steps of Tara and landed a left to his nose and a right to his solar plexus before Spelling could get off a shot. The gun clattered down the steps as Gable hit Spelling with two more to the stomach. Spelling staggered backward into the front door of Tara. It gave way from five years of rot and neglect, and Spelling fell backward into shadows.

I got up and followed Gable across the porch and to the door. Spelling lay on his back in the dirt.

There was nothing behind the front wall of Tara. No rooms. No massive stairway. Just a field that led back to the next set on the back lot over a little hill. That's the way it had been five years ago and the way it was now.

I know. Gable knew and even Spelling knew that Hollywood was the work of people who knew how to build dreams. Phil wasn't out in the darkness and neither was much of Selznick International, which was in big money trouble and already selling its lot and land back to R.K.O.

"You parked far?" I asked.

"Over the hill," said Gable, adjusting his cap.

"Why don't you take off? I'll take Spelling in. He may rant about seeing Clark Gable, but I'll remind the police that you're in England flying missions over Germany."

"Maybe that'd be best," he said.

"So damn close," Spelling cursed, trying to sit up. "Now, what's going to happen to me?"

"Frankly, mister," said Gable, touching the bill of his cap in mock salute, "I just don't give a damn."

The next morning Phil was a hero. Gable had made a few calls, and a general in military intelligence in Washington had called Chief Veblin of the Los Angeles Police Department and told him that Captain Philip Pevsner was getting a commendation for an undercover assignment that he had been asked to take on for the United States, an assignment that had involved a number of deaths related to top-secret protection of an air-corps officer in a key position related to the national defense. That dangerous assignment had resulted in several deaths in the past week.

I don't know how much Veblin bought, but the documents that came to him within a few days were legit. Phil saw them. Nothing Veblin could do but shake Phil's hand and send my brother back on the streets.

My tux was a mess. So were Jeremy's, Gunther's, and Shelly's. I sat down the next day in my office with Dash on the desk and tried to make up a bill. I couldn't do it. I knew Gable could pay. That wasn't the problem. The problem was I couldn't send a bill to a man who smelled like tragedy and went out to risk his life with a price on his head. It just wasn't done. Not even by cheap private investigators with small bank accounts, bad backs, miserable love lives, and a need for Wheaties.

I was going to take Dash down for tacos at Manny's. It was Sunday morning and I'd already read the *L.A. Times*, where I found a lot about the Oscars and nothing about an incident in the parking lot of the Ambassador where a man named Edgar something had died after a particularly bad performance.

The phone rang. I put down the paper, told Dash to be patient for a few more minutes, and answered the phone.

"Peters?" came a voice I thought I recognized.

"Yes," I said.

"Didn't think I'd catch you on a Sunday. Can you dance?"

"Dance?" I asked.

"You know. Fox-trot. Rumba. Waltz. Basics."

"Not so you'd recognize them, but enough to almost get by."

"Good. Good. How about meeting me tomorrow? I think I have a job you'd be particularly suited for."

"I'll give it a whirl," I said.

"I'll give you a call in the morning and set up the time and place," Fred Astaire sang, and hung up the phone.